F

-Written By-
Linette King

Published by Linette King Presents

This novel is a work of fiction. Any resemblances to actual events, real people, living or dead, organizations, establishments or locales are products of the author's imagination. Other names, characters, places, and incidents are used fictitiously.

Cover Design: Akirecover2cover
Editor: Linette King

Acknowledgement

First of all I would like to thank God who is the head of my life and household for without him I am nothing. Thank you for all you have done and all you are about to do.

To my children: Aaliyah, Alannah and Jaye! I love you more than life itself and watching you guys grow and learn is truly my greatest gift! You make me proud over and over again!

To my family: I love you guys so much! Never change.

To my readers: Thank you guys for your continuous support! I love you! I hope you enjoy!

This book is a complete work of fiction. Anything that resembles any event, person or situation is completely coincidental. It's also a rerelease!!

Table of Contents

Prologue Part 1

Zaria

"Ah fuck baby pound it! Ahhhh harder!" I screamed as Damon hit it from the back with no mercy. He had me bent over the toilet in the bathroom that was located in the hallway because I didn't have one in my bedroom. Damon reached over and placed his hand over my mouth to keep me from waking up everybody in the house.

He had been creeping over to give me the business for quite some time. Four months to be exact and nobody had a clue. At the tender age of eighteen, I still lived at home with my parents. I will be graduating next month and Damon promised me that we would be together then.

"Baby sssh you have to be quiet." He moaned in my ear. I could tell it was hard for him not to moan out with me. He had told me time and time again that I had the best pussy he had ever entered. That's saying a lot since Damon is thirty-seven years old and I'm sure he's sampled a lot of pussies in his day.

"Fuck it's so good baby." I moaned out as low as possible. I didn't know why Damon liked to sneak over here while my parents were home because he knows I'm a screamer. I don't like being quiet. Hell, I be needing to let my man know that he's giving me the business.

"Fuck girl hold on." He said as he pulled out. I frowned my face up in aggravation. I literally hated for him to pull out of me to stop his nut. You would think at his age; he would have mastered a better way to stop the nut by now.

"Don't get mad, baby that pussy is just too good." He said then sat my slim, one hundred twenty-pound frame on the sink. My frown vanished as soon as his breath tickled my pussy. I slid my ass to the edge of the sink to allow him better access.

He placed his whole mouth on my pussy and began to devour it! I swear it felt like he was performing an exorcism on it or something! I wrapped my long legs around his neck then used my arms to push my body closer to his face. He cupped my ass in his hands as I ground my hips into his face.

"Ah fuck baby eat that shit baby!" I coached because he was the truth in every way! I've had boyfriends before and I used to let them finger me but they've never sampled it. Damon was my first, my one and only and maybe that's why I was so in love with everything about him. The way he laid the dick down was amazing and his head game was ridiculous!

I could feel my legs shaking as my orgasm came to a peak. He started to suck hard on my clit as he fingered me. I tried to grind into his face because I was having trouble releasing that orgasm.

"Cum for me baby." He said then started back sucking. "I'm trying." I moaned out because I could feel it coming it just wouldn't release. "Ugh!" I moaned out in frustration. Damon lowered my body and slammed into me.

He started to slow wind and massage my clit as he stared into my eyes. I closed my eyes tight as I felt my nut getting closer. "Open your eyes baby." He moaned into my ear then kissed me deep and passionately.

I opened my eyes and looked into his. "I love you." I said to him as he continued to stare into my eyes and grind slow but deep. He was hitting my spot and I closed my eyes again. "No look at me." He said so I forced my eyes back open.

"I love you." I repeated and he smiled a bright beautiful smile. "Cum with me." He said as he continued to grind as he played with my clit. I stared at him and matched each stroke until we came at the same time.

I have no clue why I always let him cum inside of me because I'm not on birth control. Maybe it's the love that I have for him that allows me to make such dumb decisions. We have sex every time he sneaks over and every time it's unprotected. He may not even be able to have children.

He placed me upright on the sink with his dick still buried inside of me. I placed my arms around his neck and kissed him again. My juices tasted so sweet on his lips and tongue. I laid my head on his shoulder and tried to savor the moment.

"Baby I gotta go." He said and reality hit me all at once. I was so tired of sneaking Damon in my parent's house only for him to fuck my brains out and go back home. I had never even been to his house because of the neighborhood that he lives in.

I don't understand why he won't just move out of that neighborhood and find us a place together. "You always have to go." I whispered as I pushed him away from me. His now limp dick dangled between his legs.

I hopped down and almost hit the floor because my legs felt like noodles. Damon reached out to help balance me but I knocked his hands away. "Don't fucking touch me!" I snapped at him then made my way to take a quick shower before I snuck him right back out.

"Baby don't be like that." He said as he tried to step into the shower with me for another round. I shot him a look so cold it stopped him dead in his tracks. I snatched the shower curtain back so hard that I snatched it completely off the rod!

He chuckled softly then began to put his clothes on as I washed up. I was mad and embarrassed but the only emotion he was about to get was anger. After my shower, I dried quickly and threw my clothes on. I opened the door and peaked my head out. The coast was clear.

"Let's go." I said as I walked out of the bathroom and headed straight for the back door. He always parked on the street behind our house and just cut through the backyard to get over here.

"Baby you gone chill with the attitude? You know I'm going to come back." He said to me as I walked with him across the yard and over to his car. I shook my head and folded my arms over my chest. I didn't have time for this bullshit. It's been four months too long of the same shit and I was ready to call it quits.

"I'll be back." he said as he got in his truck. "Don't bother. I'm done." I said then turned to walk away. He hopped out of the car and grabbed me before I made it past the front of his big ass F250 all black truck.

"Don't be like that Z. You know I need you in my life." He pleaded with a sincere look on his face. "Do you want to be with me?" I asked because I believe that if he wanted to be with me, we wouldn't have to be a secret. Hell it's been four months and we haven't even established what we are doing!

"Yes baby the timing just isn't right. I have to get my life tog-"

"Get your life together?! Nigga you are thirty-seven years old if you ain't got it together by now then it won't get together!" I snapped then turned to walk away. "And neither will we." I threw over my shoulder. I didn't know what he needed to get together but I did know that I wasn't waiting any longer.

Prologue Part 2

Arteal

"Mom, I'm sorry please stop!" I screamed as she swung the belt over and over again. At eighteen years old I should not be subjected to this foolishness. I looked up at her with tears streaming down my face and she beat me unmercifully.

"No don't yell stop now lil hoe! You wasn't yelling stop when you and that lil nigga was fucking in my shit!" she yelled out just as she threw the belt down on the floor and started to wail on me with her fists.

As many times as I'd snuck people in, I had never been caught before. I wish I could still say that because I promise I'm never doing that shit again. She's always home so it's not like I can wait until she leaves to sneak anyone in.

It likes once my no good ass daddy left, I was beyond happy but she's been so down that she doesn't ever do anything for herself. I know that she was disappointed in me when she walked out of her room and heard me moaning.

Truth be told if the damn CD didn't skip when it did she wouldn't have heard me anyway. Terrance wasn't the first guy that I snuck in but he will for damn sure be the last one. What I didn't have time for was this beating that she was giving me.

I should have learned by now that she's triggered easily now that my dad is gone. It doesn't take much at all for her to get physical. Hell I can forget to cut a light off and she will come in swinging. It had never been this bad before though.

She finally got tired enough to walk out of the room and I could finally catch my breath. I hoped like hell Terrance didn't go to school and tell anyone what transpired. My thoughts went back to just a few hours earlier.

"Hello?" I answered the phone on speakerphone because I had just gotten out of the shower. I was completely out of breath because I had to rush out of the shower and dry my hands off enough to answer.

"You started without me?" Terrance joked over the phone. I smiled as I looked down at my freshly shaven pussy and stuck two fingers inside and moaned my response to him. I turned the water on so my mom wouldn't walk past the bathroom door and hear me.

"Girl you got my dick hard as fuck! I'm fina pull up." He said then hung the phone up. I lotioned my body up quickly and threw a shirt on to open the door before he had a chance to knock. Terrance didn't know that we wouldn't be completely alone and I didn't want to miss any dick so I didn't want him to find out.

I treaded lightly across the cheap carpet in our house until I made it to the front door. I opened it just as he held his hand up to knock on the door. Talk about being right on time!

He rushed in and began to kiss me passionately as he slipped his hand under my shirt while kicking the door shut. The kiss threw me completely off because we don't do no kissing. I still wanted to fuck though so I just pulled away and grabbed his hand.

Once we made it into my room, I hit play on an old crunk jams mixtape. I removed my shirt, turned around and dropped down to my knees so I could unbuckle his pants and take him into my mouth.

He stopped me and unbuckled them himself and stepped completely out of them before he guided me to the bed. He pushed me down and spread my legs. I couldn't wait for him to enter me. I needed this fix because thoughts of my past had been coming back heavy lately.

He blew softly on my pussy and tears streamed down into my ears instantly. I wanted him to stop but I didn't want to seem weird about the whole thing. It always started this way and I always hated it but I needed to be in control. I wiped my eyes then pushed his head from between my legs.

"You didn't like it?" he asked with a slight hint of disappointment in his voice. I knew he liked me but I don't think I'm capable of having anything real after what I'd been through. Either that or I just hadn't decided to open myself up to it yet.

"I'm just ready to feel you inside of me." I said as I stood up and pushed him on the bed. His dick stood straight up like it was saluting me. I pushed the thoughts of the past to the back of my mind as I waited for him to put a condom on.

"What's the hold up baby?" he asked and I gave him the side eye. He knows what happened the last time we had sex raw and ended up at the damn

clinic! Zaria still curses me out about that and it was months ago!

"You need a condom T."

"I'll pull out this time." He responded then grabbed me and pulled me to him. Before I could protest, he was on top of me and began to kiss on my neck. That was one of my major spots so I was beyond ready for it.

He slid into me slowly at first because it had been so long. After my abortion, I was told not to have sex for six weeks and just to be on the safe side I waited eight. I felt every inch of him inside of me and that's exactly what I needed.

Before long, my legs were shaking as he rammed his dick into me like he had something to prove. "Ah fuck! Harder!" I yelled as the CD skipped a beat.

"What the fuck?" I heard my mom say but I was too focused on the nut that I was about to get.

"Don't stop! What are you doing?!" I snapped after he pulled out of me. I opened my eyes in time to see my mom pulling Terrance out of my room. "Oh shit." I exclaimed as I hopped off the bed and ran out into the hallway.

She hit him over and over as she made her way to the door and pulled him along the way. He fell several times until he was tossed outside with no pants, boxers or shoes. I could only imagine how embarrassed he was. I just hope he didn't tell anyone.

When she closed the door she turned her assault on me.

It took her two fucking hours to get tired and walk away from me. She'll never have to worry about this happening ever again. Hell I'm going to obey her and the man that raped me for years and not give the pussy away to anyone.

I crawled under my covers and cried for about fifteen more minutes. I could feel myself drifting off to sleep but I was afraid that she may only be taking a break and would be back to finish her attack so fear kept me awake.

She walked into my room with a screwdriver and took my doorknob off. It wasn't until I crept out of my room to use the bathroom that I saw she had removed the doorknobs off every door except for her room door.

Chapter 1

Zaria

"What's wrong girl you been in the bathroom all morning?" my best friend Arteal asked as she stood next to me with my hair in her hand as I threw up in the bathroom at her house. I would have locked the door, but there is no freaking door knob on the door.

I gave her a shoulder shrug although I had a feeling that I was pregnant. I bought a pregnancy test but I didn't want to find out on graduation day. This was supposed to be a joyous day, not one filled with dread, doom and vomit.

"I know you ain't pregnant because you're single and still a virgin right?" she stated but it actually sounded more like a question. Like maybe she needed verification because she knew that her best friend would tell her if it was anything other than what she had stated.

I hadn't told a soul about Damon and I because I made a promise to him that I wouldn't but I haven't talked to him in a month. I was serious about being done because I didn't have time for the foolishness that came with him. All of that sneaking in and out of my parent's house just wasn't called for.

I stood up and brushed my teeth without answering the question. I am a horrible liar and I know Arteal will see straight through my bullshit so the best thing for me to do right now is ignore her. After I brushed my teeth, we went back to Arteal's room to get dressed.

"So Twan is having a graduation party tonight are you down?" she asked as if I haven't been throwing my life up in her toilet all morning. I rolled my eyes at her and slipped on a navy blue and peach striped maxi dress that my mom bought me from Ross.

"Did you not just see how sick I am?" I asked with a slight frown on my face. I could feel more vomit coming up but I knew it was only going to be that yellow stuff. I burped softly and could taste it all in my mouth. Arteal frowned her face up in disgust.

"You know what, I'm fina give you one of these pills my mama got for nausea." She said then walked out of the room. I sat down on the bed and slipped on my shoes and grabbed my cap and gown. Arteal had been dressed since 8 this morning and we don't have to be there until 10 and the ceremony starts at 11.

"Here go ahead and take it so we can go bitch its fifteen minutes til." She said as she handed me the pill and a bottle of water. I swallowed it and grabbed my purse then headed behind her towards the front door.

"Catch ya later ma!" Arteal yelled through her mother's closed door. "Alright I'm going to catch Tammy and Dank." Ms. Rita yelled back. Tammy and Dank are my parents and they've been together all of my life. Well on and off all of my life and they still aren't married but aye to each its own right?

"So party or no party?" Arteal asked as we pulled off and headed down the street. I felt my phone vibrate in my clutch so I pulled the phone out and checked it. I didn't recognize the number so I went ahead and answered it.

"Congratulations baby I miss you so much." Damon said into the receiver. I rolled my eyes and sighed heavily. "You have the wrong number." I said then hung the phone up and blocked that number too. I have had to block his cell phone number along with two other numbers so far and he obviously still had not gotten the picture.

"Let's party." I said then turned the music up. Rihanna's song work was on and we jammed all the way to our school's stadium. My nerves were on edge as Arteal and I went our separate ways so we could take our seats. Everyone else was already seated due to the fact that it was now a little after ten so we were late.

"Thanks for joining us, beautiful." Kyle, one of the coolest, craziest guys in our class said to me once I took my seat next to him. It was never a dull moment whenever Kyle was around so I knew it was going to be hard to stay quiet throughout the ceremony. Plus nobody in our class was a stick in the mud and we'd probably all have community service after this in order to receive our diploma.

"Oh hush nigga and you better not get me in trouble!" I said to him with a smile. "Now that I can't promise you." He said then winked at me. I shook my head and played with my phone until graduation started.

All of the parents were asked to remain quiet until every student's name was called but of course nobody listened. It made the graduation longer than it needed to be because we had to wait until the noise died down before the next name was called.

Once graduation was over, I was surprised to see that nobody got in trouble even though damn near everybody danced across the stage. The medicine Arteal gave me worked because I didn't feel like throwing up at all.

"Can you believe we did it?" Arteal screamed in my face as she jumped up and down. "I don't know how we made it, I'm just glad we did." I said as I pulled my gown off only to be smacked on the ass repeatedly. "ASS, ASS, ASS, ASS, ASS." Kyle sang

Big Sean's song and popped as he did so. I frowned at him but couldn't help but laugh along with Arteal.

"Yall going to Twan's party?" he asked and I gave him a head nod. "Keep that on fam!" he said and I shook my head. He walked off and Arteal and I headed towards our parents who had just walked onto the field with us.

"Baby you are glowing so I know how happy you are. You guys look beautiful." My mom said with tears falling down her cheeks. It wasn't nothing for her to cry about because it isn't like I'm going to college or anything like that. I hate school so I'm definitely not going to college and paying for it.

"Thanks ma."

"Thanks Ms. Tammy."

I looked over at my dad who hadn't said a word. He just stared at me as if he could see through my soul. I sure as hell hope he couldn't see the child that may be growing inside of his little girl. He'd kill Damon if he knew he had been sleeping with me especially in his house so hopefully I'm not pregnant. I hope I have a little virus or something.

"Ok let's go eat together and then you guys can go hang out with your friends." My mom suggested and we all left.

Chapter 2

Arteal

I was beyond ecstatic to be done with school! We had finally done it. With all of the shit I'd gone through growing up, I still made it through school. I can't wait until I go off to college too. The last thing I wanted to do was hang around here with people that will be stuck doing the same shit they'd been doing the last four years of high school.

I've had so much time on my hands not having sex these last few months that I've had no choice but to get to know myself. The hardest part of it all was not being able to confront the man that almost ruined my life.

The sad part about it is, I'd never told a soul what was going on. I felt disgusted. I knew what my dad was doing to me was wrong but I didn't want people to look at me crazy for allowing him to do it so I kept it to myself.

Whenever he would come in my room and do unspeakable things to my body, he'd always tell me to never give the pussy away to anyone else and that's why after he left, that's exactly what I did. I began to pride myself on defying him because that was the only control I had.

I didn't know what else I was supposed to do. My only problem now is, I don't know where he is or how to find him. Then I don't want to go alone because he may do it again. I want Zaria to come with me but that means I'd have to tell her what he did to me first.

I love Zaria to the moon and back but she's a virgin so she won't understand why I had sex with my father. I don't want her to look at me differently so I pretend like nothing's wrong. Not just for her. I pretend for everyone that may be watching.

I have to pretend that I'm ok because they have no clue that I'm really dying inside. I'm trying desperately to hold it together but I don't think I can do it on my own anymore. I need somebody, anybody.

That's why when Twan showed interest in me I decided to open up and give in to being his friend on a whatever happens, happens basis. The sad part is, I'm afraid to open completely up because he may not want me anymore.

I've had sex with so many people since my dad left that I don't keep count anymore. I stopped counting at eight. At first it was just boys at our school, but then it went to just boys wherever I could find them.

I'm not gay, but I've even had a little fun with a few girls. Jade has a fade and she used a strap so I guess it wasn't like I was doing anything anyway.

"What's on your mind?" my mom Rita asked as we rode together to go eat before Zaria and I made our way to Twan's party. I wanted to tell my mom on so many occasions why I am the way I am but I feel like it's too late.

Plus, he's already gone now and telling her what he did to me won't change the fact that it happened to me. It doesn't matter how bad I didn't want it to happen or how my mom shouldn't have let it happen or how my dad shouldn't have made it happen because the truth remains the same, it happened.

"Nothing, just happy to be free." I said to her and she nodded her head. She looked over at me like she knew there was more but my mom has never been one to push the issue.

There had been times that I'd been crying because my dad had just forced himself inside of me again and she would walk in to see what was wrong. I'd just say nothing and even though I know she knew I was lying, she never pushed the issue.

"I'm proud of you baby." She said then turned the music up. I nodded my head to the beat of the song I had never heard before. I felt just like the chick singing the song too because just like her, I was crashing and I too needed a miracle.

About ten minutes later we pulled up to the restaurant that we had to eat at with our family before I would get to see Twan. I don't know what it was about him but I liked it. For the first time, I wanted to actually get to know him. Giving him my body hadn't crossed my mind.

I walked over to the door and held it open for my mom, Ms. Tammy and Dank. Zaria eyed me as I smiled at her. I knew she didn't really want to go to the party but I had a surprise for her little virgin ass.

One of our classmates told Twan that he wanted just one chance with Zaria and after that, if it didn't work out, he'd leave her alone. They were already friends so I don't know why he needed me to break the ice for him. Especially as funny as he is.

We were seated and I noticed that the entire time, Zaria's dad kept staring at her. My thoughts went back on my dad and I just hoped like hell that he wasn't doing to Zaria what my dad had done to me. The thought alone made me so sick that I had to excuse myself.

I walked slowly to the bathroom and tried to rid myself of the thoughts. For so long, having sex was the only thing that kept my mind busy enough. Now I was stuck with nothing. When I made it inside of the bathroom, I washed my hands then splashed some water on my face.

I pulled out my little stash that I kept in the shallow end of my lipstick and dumped a small amount of what I like to call peace between my thumb and index finger. I looked up at my reflection because I couldn't believe what I had become.

"Fuck it." I said then snorted the cocaine. As I stared at my reflection, I debated on whether or not I should do another bump. I knew what I had just taken was enough to calm my nerves but I also knew that the feeling wouldn't last.

I didn't know how much more I could take of the constant thoughts before I broke down and started free fucking again. That's why I resorted to this. I needed an escape. I literally hate my life. It's eating me up because I can be so much better than I am. I just have to figure out how to get there.

"What's wrong?" Zaria asked as she walked in the bathroom. She knew me so well but this was something that I wasn't comfortable telling her. She'd never understand. I know best friends aren't supposed to keep secrets but this is one I just can't share.

"Nothing." I said then plastered a fake smile on my face. I'd gotten so good at pretending to be happy that it was starting to look genuine to me. She nodded her head then walked over and washed her hands as well.

"Are you excited about the party?" I asked and she shook her head. Zaria never really liked being around people although she was a friendly person. She hated to go to parties so I would always have to go with my cousin Brittany and I don't fucking like her.

She thought we had so much in common because we both had fucked so many people but little did she know that I had my reasons. I don't know if she had reasons of her own but I think she just likes sex so she have it all the time.

Don't get me wrong, I like sex too but that's not at all why I have it. I think if my dad hadn't have done what he did to me, I could do without sex. I don't know how I should handle this but I know I need help. I've already passed the first step and that is admitting that I have a problem.

Now I just have to tell someone else. I'd tell Zaria if she hadn't have flipped out the way she did for that abortion. She acted like she was the father or something and I didn't give her a chance to decide if we would raise the child together or not.

I followed Zaria back to the table and my eyes zoomed in on Dank, Zaria's dad. He didn't look at her like a predator so maybe he isn't touching her. He does look like he wants to kill her though. I can't have him do either one of those though.

After we ate, my mom caught a ride with Ms. Tammy and Dank so Zaria and I could head to the party. I didn't care, I was just glad that I didn't have to drive her all the way home first.

Chapter 3

Zaria

That was the most awkward lunch I'd ever had with my dad staring a mud hole through me the entire time. I was too afraid to ask him any questions because I didn't want my questions to lead to him having questions that I wasn't able to answer.

"So what's up with your dad?" Arteal asked and I gave her a shoulder shrug because I wasn't ready to talk about it with her either. I wanted to just brush it off as my dad being nervous about my freedom or life decisions now but I can't say.

"I'm nervous about this party." I lied just to change the subject. Arteal gave me a weird look and I knew she didn't believe me. We tied in class favorite so she knew I got along with everyone and everybody loved both of us so there was no reason for me to be nervous.

"Girl please and you know Kyle likes you right?" she asked and that was the first time I'd heard of that so I shook my head. I've known Kyle since grade school and not once had he ever given me a reason to think he liked me.

"How you know?" I asked because I hope she had more to go on than him popping me on the butt after graduation because he's always doing something off the wall. You can't even say he likes me because he called beautiful. That came about when we all hung out one day and this guy wanted to know my name. Well we had just watched that movie “you got served” so I copied off the character “Beautifull” remember the two L’s.

“I overheard him telling Twan. He’s going to make his move at the party.” She said and my eyes bucked open. He was a good looking guy but I had never taken him seriously before so I don’t think I’ll be able to now.

We’d blend perfectly though with my caramel complexion and his smooth chocolate skin and perfect white teeth. “Oh gosh.” I thought to myself once I actually pictured him. It’s crazy how I never looked at Kyle like that before now. “Shit I’m really nervous now.” I thought to myself.

“I’m not going to mess up our friendship.” I said to Arteal and she rolled her eyes. “Girl live a little! Get ya lil pussy licked on or something you don’t know what you’re missing!” she said to me with a smile. “I know exactly what I’m missing because I’ve had it and I’m missing it.” Is what I wanted to say. “Girl please whatever.” Is what actually came out.

We turned on Twan’s street and it was packed already. “Man I hope all that food I ate doesn’t come up.” I said as Arteal found a parking spot and began to reapply her lip gloss. “I thought you would say that." She said as she handed me another pill. I smiled and swallowed It without anything to drink.

I checked my make up and smiled at myself. I was truly a beautiful girl and my mom was right, my skin had a slight glow to it. "Ready?" she asked and I gave her a head nod then exited out of the car. We walked hand in hand down the street until we reached Twan's house.

There were so many people there that the party had people in the front yard, backyard and inside of the house. I saw Kyle chopping it up with Twan and made my way over to speak. This was about as bold as I had ever been because I normally let guys approach me when they want to speak or have any type of conversation.

"Hey you guys." I spoke and reached over to give Twan a hug. He returned the gesture and gave me a head nod. I reached over to hug Kyle and he pulled me in close to him and grabbed my ass. I could feel his dick pressed up against my stomach as I looked up into his eyes.

Never before had Damon and I been able to do anything like this in front of people. We hugged all the time but only in my parent's bathroom so it felt different to be able to do this and not have to hide it. I looked up at him and smiled.

"Well damn that was fast!" Arteal said as she walked up. She had stopped to speak with someone else before she joined us. I laughed and turned around then gave her a playful shove. Kyle pulled me close to him and wrapped his arms around me from behind.

"Aye, aye none of that! Won't be making no babies over here!" Twan's dad walked out of the house and joked with us playfully. He dapped Twan up and gave him a head nod. "Aye dad I want you to meet your future daughter in law." Twan said then pulled Arteal close to him.

Her bright skin turned red from embarrassment and her hand flew to her mouth. "Nice to meet you young lady. I didn't even know my son was dating anyone." He said then looked over at Twan. "We aren't dating." She said softly then turned around and looked at me.

I fell out laughing and so did Kyle and Twan. Twan's dad stood there with a confused look on his face. "She's your future daughter in law dad. I didn't say anything about us dating right now." Twan said as if that made sense. How the hell does he know they will get married if they hadn't even started dating.

Twan's dad shook his head and walked away. I didn't notice he had a microphone in his hand until he cleared his throat. "I need everyone to make their way to the front yard I have an announcement." He said over the microphone.

He gestured for Twan to come stand next to him and Twan pulled Arteal with him. I laughed so hard tears were coming from my eyes. Arteal looked like they were about to sell her or something. I had no idea why she was so afraid but you could see it all over her face.

"I just wanted to congratulate the entire class of 2016 for your big accomplishment. YOU MADE IT!" Twan's dad yelled and everyone went crazy yelling as well. I totally saw where Twan got his loud and obnoxious behavior from. He waited for us to quiet down before he continued.

"I was so proud of my son that my brother and I decided to go half on him a 2012 Lexus." He said then pointed down the street. Twan's uncle drove slowly down the street in the white car that had a red bow wrapped around the front of it.

Everyone went wild like it was their gift or something. Kyle picked me up and placed me around his neck and did a light jog over to where Twan and Arteal stood. I was so stuck on not falling that I didn't notice who his uncle was until everybody got quiet.

I lifted my head slowly and looked directly at Damon who stood outside of the car and stared directly at me. I can only imagine how confused everyone was so I played along like I was confused too. I looked behind me and everything as if I too was looking for the person that had Damon's attention.

"C'mon boy, what you waiting on?!" Damon said once he realized that he was staring at me. I sighed noticeably and tapped Kyle on his head. He put me down in front of him and kissed me on the forehead. I swear I never knew how affectionate he was.

Twan left Arteal where she stood and ran off to dap Damon up and hop in the car. He sped off without a second thought and left everyone at his party standing in the front yard not knowing what to do next. "Is the party over?" I asked Kyle and he gave me a shoulder shrug.

He pulled me away from the crowd. "What was that about?" he asked as he looked down into my eyes. "What?" I asked as I feigned ignorance. I knew exactly what he was talking about but I wasn't sure if we should be having this conversation right now.

He looked back at Damon having a conversation with Twan's dad and back at me. "If we gone build something then we need to start off right. I have no reason not to trust you so don't give me that reason." Kyle said and I had never heard him that serious.

"Let's go inside." I said and pulled him into the house behind me.

Chapter 4

Arteal

I think I was just as confused as everyone else when Twan's uncle got out of the car that Twan had just gotten for graduation and stared at Zaria. All I know is I'm not a dummy so I know they know each other but I don't know how.

I watched Kyle pull her over to the side so I knew that he was trying to figure out how they knew each other too.

"What you looking at beautiful?" Twan's dad asked once I focused my attention back on Twan who hopped in his car and pulled off like I wasn't just standing here with him. It was rude as fuck if I may say so myself but I guess the excitement was overwhelming.

"Nothing. Just seeing where Zaria went." I said as I turned around just in time to see her heading inside of the house with Kyle. I wanted to run inside but Twan's dad stopped me.

"Mind your business young lady." He said as if he knew something that I didn't. I frowned my face up in confusion then looked down at my phone.

"Damon what was all that about." Twan's dad asked. I sucked my teeth because he'd just told me to mind my own business and now he is trying to figure out the same thing that I wanted to know. I wish I hadn't sucked my teeth because the sound caused Damon to look at me.

"Let's go over here and chop it up." Twan's dad said then they both walked away. I sighed because I was now alone and I knew what happened every time I was alone. My phone vibrated in my hand. I welcomed the brief distraction.

Twan: walk down da street and ride with me

Arteal: no cme back 2 ur party

I placed the phone back in my pocket and decided to go see where Zaria and Kyle had run off too. As soon as I walked inside of the house, I could hear faint noises coming from the bathroom.

"She's finally getting her little coochie licked on." I laughed to myself just as I heard people talking near the back door.

I had no clue what I was supposed to do in this situation and I could feel myself getting antsy. I made my way into the kitchen and grabbed a plate so I could pretend like I was about to fix something to eat. I knew I needed to stay put to distract anyone that needed to use the bathroom until they finished.

After I made sure that the coast was clear, I reached down in my pocket and pulled out my lipstick. This was beginning to be a daily habit when I started off only using it when I couldn't have sex.

As I snorted it off my hand, I wiped my nose and tilted my head back. It felt so good to be back in a state of euphoria. My thoughts reflected back to the night I snorted my first line.

"Please Zaria come out with me. I have our fake IDs ready." I pleaded although I knew that it didn't matter how much I begged Zaria to go out she would find some dumb excuse why she couldn't make it this time.

"Girl, I'm tired. I've been studying all day." She lied because we both knew that she had never been the studying type. Hell she didn't even like school. I pinched the bridge of my nose to attempt to

calm myself down because I just didn't understand why she never wanted to go out.

"Guess I'll call Brittany." I said then hung the phone up before she could respond. I didn't want to hear a thing unless she was changing her mind about going. I debated heavily on rather or not I should call my too hot to trot cousin.

That chick was smashing almost every guy our age and the ones she wasn't smashing, I was so I guess I can't judge her too much. I shook my head because I couldn't believe that I had to hang out with her again. I sighed and placed the call to her.

"Hey cuzzo!" Brittany exclaimed. I hated when she did that fake shit because we both know that she doesn't like me. The feeling is mutual too. The only difference is, I never pretend like I like her. She's fun to hang out with but she's messy as hell so I will only hang out with her on a social basis.

"Let's go out."

"Cool, come scoop me." she responded and I smiled. It was always just that simple with Brittany. Our conversation went like that every time. Neither of us had kids so it wasn't like we needed time to find a sitter.

I got dressed and left the house. My dress was so short that I could have put pants on and worn it as a shirt. The goal was to make everyone want to fuck just as bad as I did. I was all for a one night stand.

When I pulled up to Brittany's one bedroom, income based apartment she was already sitting outside. When she noticed me, she stood up and made her way over to my car and hopped in. Her dress stopped right above her knees but it showed every curve. She looked good.

We headed to the club and waited in the long line because we didn't have money to go through the VIP line so we had to stand in the general admissions line. Ladies always got in free before twelve so we always made sure to show up before then because neither one of us worked.

Once we got in the club, I started to dance immediately. Brittany ended up leaving me to dance alone after this guy came and got her off the dance floor. I danced two songs straight by myself before I decided to find a seat.

"Leaving so soon?" I heard a male voice ask in my ear. I looked down at his hand that was locked firmly around my upper arm. He released his grip and held his hands up in a surrender fashion and smiled.

I took that time to admire his perfect white teeth and amazing physique. Before that very moment, I had never looked at a white man twice but this man came straight from heaven and was right on time for me.

We slow grinded to three songs straight and I was ready to have my first taste of a white man. He hadn't even told me his name and he didn't know mine but I allowed him to lead me out of the club and out back to a newer model volkswagen.

As soon as we got in the backseat, he began to place soft, delicate kisses all over my body. I knew I was beyond sweaty but maybe that's what he liked. He raised my dress slowly and began to kiss around my pantyline. My thoughts jumped back to what had been done to me.

I pulled my legs back and scooted to the other side of the car. He looked at me with a confused look on his face before it went blank. "I know what you need." he said as he leaned his frame across the seat to reach inside of the glove compartment.

He sprinkled a little bit on the area between his thumb and index finger then held his hand out to me. I shook my head and he gave me a shoulder shrug before he snorted it off his hand. He sat down and leaned his head back against the seat.

He looked so relaxed and at peace that I leaned over and took the small vial out of his hand and sprinkled a little bit on my hand and did exactly what he had done. I'd never been so happy in my life.

I glanced over at him just as he pulled his meat out and began to stroke it. I wasted no time taking him in my mouth. It was salty but I didn't give a damn at that moment. He pushed me back and entered me slowly as he groaned out.

The drug enhanced every feeling and I enjoyed every bit of what he was doing to me.

"Hey you not gonna fix the plate?" Amber asked and snapped me out of my thoughts. I could feel my panties were wet when I stepped out of the way. I had been trying to find that man ever since to get what he gave me.

When I couldn't find him, I had to settle for what Andrew, one of the corner boys by my house had and it was watered down compared to what my white man gave me that night at the club. I had yet to experience that high since then.

The sound of soft cries brought me back to reality. Nothing he's doing to her should have her crying! I made my way to the bathroom and tried to listen carefully at first so I'd know what to do. I tried to hype myself up because Kyle is a pretty big dude and if he's hurting her, I'll need help helping her.

"Fuck." I thought as I paced the floor outside of the door. My nose had started running so I used the back of my hand to wipe the snot away as I waited for the perfect chance to knock on the door.

Chapter 5

Zaria

I sat next to Kyle on the couch in a position where I could see if anyone entered and knew when to quit talking. I took a deep breath and got ready to tell him something I hadn't even told my best friend yet. I knew she would kill if she found out that I told someone else something first. Hell she's going to be mad that I didn't tell her the moment after everything happened.

"I met him about seven months ago. We talked for a while and exchanged numbers." I began but Kyle's facial expression stopped me from talking instantly. His face was all screwed up and it kind of scared me because I didn't know what to expect.

"Why'd you stop?" he asked with his face still balled up. "Because of the way you're looking at me." I said and his facial features softened. "It's not you Zaria, it's him so keep talking." He said and confused me but I decided to just continue anyway.

"Well after talking on the phone for two months I started to sneak him in my parents house. For four months he snuck over whenever he could until I broke things off." I kept it short and sweet. I didn't need to tell Kyle how Damon devoured this pussy and taught me how to deepthroat him.

"Why did you end it?" he asked as he stared at me intently. I thought about it for a second. I didn't know how petty it sounded and I actually cared what Kyle thought about me. That's why I decided to tell him the truth.

"We had to keep us a secret and I deserved more." I stated simply. "How could he go public with someone that's young enough to be his daughter?"

Kyle asked with his head tilted to the side as if he really wanted me to answer that question. The only reason I answered it is because I felt some type of way about it.

"Age ain't nothing but a number." I responded with a roll of my neck. "Yea with damn near twenty numbers in between." Kyle said and my mouth hung open in disbelief. I didn't want to talk about this anymore and I think I just lost Kyle.

I gave him a head nod and stood to my feet. "Don't walk away from me Zaria." He said. I stopped and turned around only to see that he had stood up as well. "I thought you were done with me." I stated honestly.

"I didn't say that, did I?" he asked and I turned back around. "Well there's more." I said as I dug in my purse and pulled the pregnancy test halfway out of my purse so he could see what I was getting at.

He blew out a frustrated breath and looked at me with so much disappointment that I had to look away. "Why haven't you taken it?" he asked and I gave him a shoulder shrug. He grabbed my arm and pulled me towards the bathroom.

My nerves kicked into overdrive as he opened the bathroom door and gave me a light shove inside. Once I was in the bathroom, he closed the door and left me to do my thing in peace. "Oh God please don't let me be pregnant by this man." I said as I squat over the stick.

Once I was done, I placed the stick on top of toilet paper on the sink, cleaned myself and paced the bathroom floor. Those were the longest two minutes of my life. I stopped walking just long enough to look at the test results.

Tears clouded my vision as I looked at those two lines. I began to cry so loud that Kyle burst through the door and immediately wrapped me in his arms. He sat on the toilet and pulled me on his lap and just let me cry.

A knock at the door ceased my tears as realization of where I am kicked in. "What's going on in there?" Arteal asked and I sighed a big breath of relief. I opened the door and pulled her inside with us. "What the hell yall-"

When she saw the pregnancy test on the sink she stopped talking and peered over at the lines. She turned around and looked between me and the test then shook her head. "You pregnant?" she asked and I nodded my head as the tears continued to flow.

“Ssssh ssssh it's ok. I got your back.” She said and I cried harder. Kyle stormed out of the bathroom. I shook my head and hugged Arteal tight as I cried on her shoulder. “Who?” she asked and I looked at her and gave her the same story I’d just given Kyle.

“He took advantage of you boo. You never went to his house?” she asked and I shook my head.

“Well he’s probably married or something.” She said and my heart dropped down in my stomach. She grabbed the clean end of the pregnancy test and wrapped the whole thing in tissue then stuck it in my purse.

“It’s time to pay his wife or girlfriend whatever, a little visit.” She said and pulled me out of the house.

Chapter 6

Arteal

I know I don't have room to judge anyone given the way I am but damn Zaria is a little on the dumb side. Well I take that back because I don't want to call her dumb but maybe I should call her naive.

Naw fuck that she's dumb as fuck! Why would you think anything would come out of a hidden relationship first of all? Second of all, why would you think this old ass man was going to make your young ass his woman? Third of all, why have you never been to his house?

Come on now, you've been messing with someone heavy for four months and you've never been to his house! I mean let's be real for a second and state nothing but facts! All facts, no shade!

Zaria is eighteen years old and literally just graduated from high school today. She can't cook, she doesn't have to clean and she's never had a job before in her life! She's been sneaking this man into her parent's house for four months and they've been keeping their little fling a secret.

He sold her dreams for four months but you can't even really fault him because she's grown. Hell she ain't tell me because I think she knew deep down that he was lying to her.

See we are the same type of friends when it comes to stating how we feel. We are both extremely blunt so we keep secrets for the same reason… Hearing the truth is hard to swallow.

Shit I didn't know what else to say to her other than let's pay his wife or girlfriend a visit. In all actuality I'm completely down for that but she doesn't know where the man lives so I honestly don't know how this is going to play out.

I don't want to just be following the man around to a bad neighborhood since that's why he told her he'd never invited her over. That had to be some bullshit though. He has to have someone already in his life and he can't go public with them both.

I grabbed Zaria's arm before we made it out of the door and pulled her all the way back into the bathroom. We needed to have a heart to heart while I knew everything so I could let her know that she would feel a whole lot worse before she felt better.

"First of all, are you keeping this baby?" I asked but at the same time I knew she better had said yes because of how she did me when I had an abortion.

"I don't know." she said as she shook her head. She looked down at the floor and I could see her tears falling on her arms. This may not have been the time to tear into her but I'll be damned if I don't give her the same treatment she gave me fresh out of the clinic.

"Oh yeah? Well what happened to all that shit you were spitting at me? Did you or did you not have sex willingly and get pregnant?" I asked and she looked up at me with so much pain in her eyes that I stopped talking immediately.

"I'm sorry Arteal." she cried out and I felt like the biggest asshole ever. I didn't mean to hurt her but I had done just that. I literally felt like shit. Zaria isn't normally emotional so I guess we can blame this on the child growing inside of her.

"What are your parents going to do to you?" I asked and she gave me a shoulder shrug. Man I wanted to snort some more blow just to ease her pain for her. Shit the way she was crying, I wanted to offer her some but she can't because she's pregnant.

"What am I gonna do?" she cried out as she looked up at me. Her eyes were red and puffy. She had snot running down her nose. I reached over and grabbed some tissue so she could wipe her nose.

"You're gonna have this baby and be the best mom you can be." I said to her with a slight smile. I had to force it because I couldn't believe she was pregnant. I started to think about the way her dad was looking at her today.

"Do they know?" I asked and she shook her head. That's the only reason I can think of that her dad would be staring a mudhole in her the whole time that we ate but if she wants to stay in denial then that's on her.

"Does Damon know?" I asked and she shook her head. "Damn this bitch just ain't told nobody." I thought to myself as I ran my hand over my face. I was completely frustrated.

"C'mon let's go boo." I said then let her walk out of the door first. I waited until she was a good bit away before I sprinkled more peace on my hand and snorted it up quickly then wiped my nose. I needed to be as calm as possible to help her get through this mess.

Chapter 7

Zaria

My tear drenched face didn't catch anyone's attention as I walked out of the house because they were too engrossed in the fight that was taking place on the lawn. I walked closer to the fight and my eyes widened when I realized the fight was between Kyle and Damon.

Damon was on the ground by the time we made it outside with Kyle on top of him sending blows to his head. I didn't know what to do and I looked to Twan's dad for help but he was getting a kick out of the whole situation.

"Twan do something!" I yelled but he looked like he didn't have a clue what to do. I was beyond frantic. I didn't know what to call Kyle but he was beating the dog shit out of Damon whom I also didn't know what to call.

"Oh gosh STOP!" I yelled but my words fell on deaf ears. Nobody stopped fighting. They continued to go blow for blow with no interference from anybody. I looked back at Arteal and she had an oddly calm expression on her face. When she noticed that I was looking at her it was as if she could read my mind because she shook her head at me.

I turned around and waited for the perfect opportunity to try and break the fight up. They were fighting over me anyway so I may as well be the person that breaks it up. I waited a few more seconds with hopes that someone would intervene before I did.

I looked around and nobody made a move other than to get out of the way. I watched carefully and Damon had just flipped Kyle. "NO!" I yelled once Damon jumped on top of Kyle.

I ran up to the fight and grabbed Damon from behind. WHAM!

He turned around and hit me so hard that I fell backwards on my ass and tumbled over in a backwards flip. My head began to spin as I lay on my stomach completely motionless. I tried to shake the dizzy feeling but I couldn't.

"Oh shit Z I'm sorry!" Damon yelled once he realized what he had done. He grabbed me and picked me up from the ground to a standing position. He grabbed my face and touched it softly where he hit me. I moved my face out of his grasp.

I turned around and ran over to Kyle. "Are you ok?" I asked and he gave me a head nod and threw his arm over my shoulder. "Walk me to the car

I'm ready to go." I said to Kyle and we walked away with Arteal and Twan on our trail.

"You didn't have to do that, you know." I said to Kyle and he looked at me as if I was crazy. "Yes I did." He said to me and I was confused about why he thought that was something he needed to do. Kyle is only eighteen years old just like me so Damon should have never entertained a fight with him.

"He was wrong for taking advantage of you and don't say he didn't because he did. That man old as hell, he has already been with females our age because he's already been here so he already knew what you wanted. He used you Zaria and he needed to know that he was wrong." Kyle said and I understood everything that he was saying.

"You're right." I said as I looked over at Arteal. I could tell she was on cloud nine being around Twan especially since he was showing her interest. She smiled and clung to his every word as they stood a few feet away from us.

"You need to put something on your head girl. I hate to be you when you have to come up with a lie after you face your crazy ass daddy." Kyle said and my face filled with alarm. I had no idea what I was going to tell my dad. I had a whole lot of explaining to do especially when it came down to my unborn child.

I'm old enough to have an abortion but I can't afford one. Plus I know Arteal will hate me if I have one because of all the grief I gave her when she went and had one a few months ago. I had a whole lot to say about people that had abortions when I had never been in the shoes of a person who was considering it the way I am now. My thoughts about abortions have changed completely.

"I hate to be me right now. Especially being pregnant." I said and hung my head low because I had no idea what I was going to do. I could feel the tears building up as the decision weighed heavily on my heart. Kyle placed his fingers under my chin and raised my head so I would have no choice other than to look him in his eyes.

"I got you Zaria." He said and the tears began to fall. There's no way that Kyle can have my back with this child that isn't his. Especially not when he doesn't even have his own back. We both still live at home with our parents. I smiled up at him then climbed in the car.

"Call me later, Zaria." He said and I gave him a head nod. We've had each other's number for as long as I can remember because we've been friends all of our lives.

Chapter 8

Damon

Now understand this before you go to turning your damn nose up at me. Zaria is grown and she's been grown since I've known her. The only thing I was wrong for was leading her on when I had my own situation but I honestly just couldn't get enough of her.

Zaria's pussy gripped my dick like nothing I'd ever felt before and she had no problem getting wet. I was so used to using lube that her natural wetness sent me over the edge. Had me feeling like a crazy stalker when she cut shit off with me.

I wasn't going to ever cut anything off but I knew I had lost her. It was something about the way she walked away from me the last time that I snuck into her parents' house that let me know it was over for me.

Hell if that wasn't enough, the fact that she blocked every number that I called her from sure was. I was persistent though. I needed her back and I was going to get her back. It didn't matter what I had to do or say to get her. It's so crazy because her little young ass had me sprung. Just not sprung enough to leave what I already had.

She's never been to my house but I told her it was because of the neighborhood that I live in but that was a lie. I actually live in a pretty damn good neighborhood. My baby just has a key and I don't need Zaria walking in on some shit.

Bae is my age but we aren't official or anything either which is how I like to keep it. That way nobody can expect a commitment out of me.

Regardless of that though, I couldn't chance either one of them running into the other one.

I know women so I know if I would have allowed Zaria to come to my place to visit, that would have led to her wanting to stay the night. After staying the night she would have wanted to bring a few things with her. After that she'd want a key and I couldn't let both of them have a key. Well unless they were down for a threesome.

"You let that lil nigga hand you ya ass." my brother Brandon laughed as he walked over to me. I looked at him and shook my head as I made my way to his car. I needed him to take me to my car so I could get the hell away from these snickering mufuckers.

"Man, I wasn't expecting that. They fucking?" I asked as we made our way inside of Brandon's truck. He got a real good laugh out of that one.

"Ain't you in a relationship nigga? Don't matter who that young ass girl giving her pussy to." Brandon said as he continued to drive. I leaned my seat back and didn't respond. I just looked up at the ceiling because I couldn't believe that she would give the pussy up so fast.

"I can't believe he tried to check me man." I said and Brandon laughed. I looked over at him with a questioning look on my face. I needed to know what the fuck was so funny.

"Tried? That nigga got in that ass!" Brandon said as he continued to laugh. I shook my head because he had told the truth. It's because that nigga athletic though and I haven't worked out in years.

Truth be told I had no business tussling with somebody half my age. Especially not over a piece of pussy. That was the first time I had ever gotten into a fight over pussy. These little niggas these days need to get it together.

Shit back in my day I was fucking everybody ole lady. Shit if your lady was a victim then that was her fault because I never did more than they allowed. The same thing with Zaria. Kyle's little young ass walked up to me talking about how I took advantage of her.

I didn't do a mufucking thing to Zaria that she didn't want me to do. I had her little ass cumming all over the sink every other day and twice some days. I had her nutting all over my backseat and everything.

If he is getting the pussy he won't be getting it long because he won't be able to make her cum like

I can. He fucked around and let a real nigga get her first and now he has some real big shoes to fill.

When we made it to my car, I hopped out without another word. I needed to figure out a way back in before I lost my girl to a young nigga. She made me feel like a man every time I entered her but with Bae, I'm always pushed to the side for the person they're with.

Chapter 9

Zaria

Arteal said her goodbyes to Twan then came and got in the car. I didn't know what to do at this point. My head was hurting something serious and I was beyond aggravated. Shoot I was confused about life. Here I am fresh out of high school, still living at home with my parents, and I just found out that I'm pregnant. Life just couldn't get any more confusing.

"So are you and Kyle an item now or what?"

"With all of the drama that we've had in under twenty-four hours I doubt we'll ever be."

"Twan and I are." Arteal said with a smile as she drove back to my house. I gave her a head nod because I could already tell how funny it was going to be to watch those two be together. Now only if I could get my life together so I can get my happily ever after too.

"Are you okay?" Arteal asked and I gave her a head nod even though I wasn't sure. The last thing I wanted right now was a baby but being as though I'm pregnant right now, it's kind of too late for that. I sighed heavily and stared out of the window the rest of the way there.

We pulled up to my house and I dreaded going back inside. "I'll call you later." I said then got out of the car. I had a lot of thinking to do and I didn't need to be around anyone else at this moment. All I wanted to do was go inside, take something for my headache and lay down.

Arteal pulled off as soon as I closed the door. I swear I hate when she does that and she does it every single time! Hell even taxi cabs wait until you get inside before they pull off. I shook my head then made my way up to my porch.

I grabbed the doorknob and was snatched roughly off the porch. I tried to scream but there was a large hand pressed against my mouth. Fear gripped my soul as I was dragged off to the side of the house and through the backyard.

I bucked my body all over the place but it did nothing to stop the assailant. I bit down as hard as I could and sank my teeth down into the assailant's hand. “Aargh!” he said as he released his hold on me. I tried to break away from his grip and run but I wasn’t fast enough.

“Dammit Z stop!”

The sound of Damon’s voice stopped me dead in my tracks. I turned around slowly with shock all over my face. I could not believe he had just grabbed me from my porch like he was going to kidnap me.

“What are you doing?!” I damn near screamed. “Sssh!” he shushed me as he rushed to place his hand back over my mouth. I stepped away from him because I did not want to be near him. This isn’t the man I fell in love with. I don’t know who this man is.

“Baby I just need some of your time.” He pleaded as he grabbed a hold of my hands in his. I blinked away tears. Well I tried to but they fell anyway. I didn’t want to hear a single thing that he had to say but at the same time I wanted him to tell me something that would make me feel better.

"You used me." I cried as I stared directly at him. He shook his head and pulled me to him. "No baby no I didn't. I would never use you." He said in a pleading tone. I didn't know what to believe but it hurt less to believe him.

"You took advantage of me Damon." I said as I cried harder. "And I'm pregnant!" I cried even harder but he pulled away from me. "You pregnant?" he asked with a slight frown on his face like he didn't believe me. I nodded my head and reached in my purse to hand him the pregnancy test.

He unwrapped the tissue and a slow smile began to spread across his face. He looked up at me then scooped me up in a big hug. I didn't know how I was supposed to feel but I was happy that he was happy rather I was supposed to be or not.

"I'm gonna be a daddy?! Damn I love you!" he said.

And that did it. He had never told me he loved me before but finally, he had said it. I just looked at him because I didn't know if it was a mistake or not. He smiled at me then placed his hand on my stomach.

"You've graduated now so we can get you that apartment." My body was filled with excitement. I became overjoyed with emotion. I jumped up into his arms and we began to kiss passionately. He carried me through the yard to his car and laid my body down in the back seat of the car.

I laid perfectly still as he pulled my panties off then stuck them down in his pants pocket. He crawled on top of me and kissed the knot on my head. I knew that was his way of apologizing to me. He didn't have to apologize anymore because I knew he didn't mean to hit me.

"I've missed you so much. Don't ever leave me again." Damon said then took my pearl into his mouth. It's been so long since it had any sexual attention that I could already feel my nut rising. He stuck a finger in my pussy as he continued to suck on my clit. The sound he was making was driving me crazy and closer to my climax.

I didn't respond to his comment because I just wanted to enjoy this moment that we were having. My eyes began to roll in the back of my head as he ate me like the last supper.

"Mmmhhh I missed you." He moaned in between kisses. He stuck his stiff tongue as deep as he could in my ass and I jumped from being surprised.

He had never gone near my butt before so it caught me off guard but it felt so damn good.

“You like that?” he asked and I moaned. I was still pissed off at how our relationship had gone down the drain so quickly. All we shared was a bunch of broken promises and I didn’t want to have to deal with that again.

He sucked aggressively on my clit then stuck his finger in my butt. I didn’t know what had gotten into him but he was driving my body crazy! I could feel my orgasm building in my toes. I could tell this was about to be the biggest orgasm I had ever had in my life and I was about to ride it all the way out.

He sucked harder and stuck his finger deeper in my butt as he slipped two fingers on his other hand in my pussy. “Aaaaahhhhh Damon fuck!” I yelled out as my body rocked from the powerful orgasm that I was experiencing.

I laid on the backseat of the car with my body still trembling. If he would have blown on me again I’m sure I would have cum all over the place.

He stood up straight and unbuckled his pants and released the part of him I missed the most. I called it Mr. Guarantee because I was always guaranteed a nut.

My phone started to ring so I looked away to where it had fallen on the floor. "Kyle" flashed across the screen. I sat up quickly and looked around as guilt filled my body. We had just started to build whatever this is we were building and I was fucking up already.

"I got to go." I said to Damon as I tried to sit up only for him to push me back down. My eyes shot up to him and the look on his face made me feel horrible. He looked so hurt as he looked between me and my ringing phone. The last thing I wanted to do was hurt him.

"Don't leave me Z, I need you." He pleaded and my heart cried out for him. I looked away and he grabbed my face to force me to look up at him. He placed his lips against mine but I didn't return the gesture.

He trailed his kiss down my neck and I wanted to push him away but it felt so good. He began to spread my legs slowly as he stepped in between them. I wanted to protest hell I needed to but I didn't. He spread my lips apart as he slid into me slowly.

My breath got caught in my throat as he pumped in and out of me at a slow pace. "I love you." He said to me breathlessly. My phone started to ring again just as Damon started to pump faster. I looked down at the phone and saw that it was Kyle calling again.

"Ah fuck I'm fina cum baby." Damon said but I didn't respond. "Ungh." He grunted as he came inside of me. He pulled out, tucked his now limp dick inside of his underwear and pulled his pants back up. He smiled at me then handed me my phone.

"I gotta go Z but I'll call you later ok." Damon said then tried to kiss my lips but I turned my head in the opposite direction. I grabbed my phone, got out of the car and pulled my dress down then headed to my house without a word.

Chapter 10

Arteal

I absolutely positively could not wait to get Zaria out of my car because Terrance texted me to meet up with him. He'd finally saved up enough money to get a room. Ok don't judge me but I have to do what I have to do to stay sane.

I really didn't want the drug to take control of me so I kind of had to revert back to what I had been doing to get by. Nobody knows about Twan and I yet so until we start having sex I can just let Terrance handle my needs.

I drove like a bat out of hell and decided to take one more bump so I could enjoy every bit of dick that Terrance had to offer. I felt a bit dizzy as I pulled into the motel's parking lot like maybe I had snorted too much this time.

I leaned my head back against the seat and tried to get myself together but I could feel myself going in and out. I hoped like hell I wasn't about to die from an overdose.

"Yo, you good?" Terrance asked as he opened the door. I glanced over at him and could see how concerned he was. I didn't want him to see me like this. Man I didn't want anyone to see me like this ever.

I began to zone in and out as Terrance pulled me out of the car and carried me in the room. He laid me down in the tub and turned the cold water on, on the shower. I jumped up completely out of breath and was shocked that he would do such a thing.

"What the fuck?!" I yelled as I stood up completely drenched. My hair and clothes were completely drenched. Thank God I had on sandals or my tennis shoes would be ruined.

"Why would you do that?!" I continued to yell as I stepped out of the tub. I slipped several times and he didn't even try to help me. He simply backpedaled to the doorway and watched me with an angry expression on his face.

I pushed past him only to fall on the floor. Every time I tried to get back up I would fall right back down. I didn't understand why life kept knocking me down. I began to punch the floor over and over as the tears flowed down my cheeks.

He snatched me up roughly from the floor and tossed me on the bed. I was beyond scared and just hoped like hell that he wasn't about to rape me. I'd already been through far too much in my life to be subjected to that again.

"Were you high?" he asked through clenched teeth.

My body trembled because of how cold I was and my mouth hung open from disbelief. I literally could not believe that he had asked me that question. I mean who the fuck do he think he is to get in my personal business like that.

I climbed off the bed so I could get the hell away from him when he pushed me back down on the bed roughly. I jumped up again only for him to push me down harder. Tears flowed freely down my cheeks as my bottom lip quivered.

"Why would you do that to yourself?" Terrance asked and I could look at him and tell that he was both angry and disappointed. He walked over to my purse that sat on the floor by the bed. I watched him closely as he rummaged through it.

I just sat on the bed and watched because I knew that he would never find my stash. Just by looking at my tube of lipstick, you would never be able to tell that I kept a small stash of cocaine inside of it.

"Where is it?" he asked but I didn't respond. I was getting aggravated because I didn't come here for this. He was standing there going through my purse like he actually gave a damn. But wait…

“You want a hit?” I asked because we could definitely get it popping if we were both high. Shit that cold ass water killed my high so I’d need another bump too but it’ll only take a second.

Terrance’s eyes got wide and filled with rage just before he stormed off into the bathroom and closed the door. It wasn’t until I heard the lock click that I realized he had just taken my stash in the bathroom with him.

I ran to the bathroom and banged my fist on the door. I didn’t mind sharing but I had to decide how much I was going to give you. His ass may snort up all my shit and I didn’t have any money to get some more.

“Give me my shit!” I yelled as I banged on the bathroom door. A few minutes later he swung the door open and pushed my purse into my chest. I caught it and looked through it myself but didn’t see anything inside of it but my wallet.

“Where’s my shit?!” I asked as rage filled my body. I had spent my last on that and I needed it to last until my mom decided to give me a little bit more cash. Sure I could get a job but I’d still have to wait on a check and they would probably drug test me.

"I flushed it." he stated plainly. I dropped my purse and rushed past him. I dropped down to my knees in front of the toilet then stuck my hand in as far as I could. Tears escaped my eyes as I tried desperately to grab something that I already knew was long gone.

"You look pathetic." Terrance said from the doorway. "Fucking eighteen year old junkie." he continued and I attacked him.

"I'm not a junkie!" I yelled as I swung at him over and over. He grabbed me up in a tight bear hug and the fight was over just that quick. "I'm not a junkie." I repeated because I knew he didn't believe me.

"You trying to convince me or yourself?" he asked sarcastically without releasing me. I stopped resisting because he had begun to squeeze me tighter. I thought about his sarcastic question but I know I'm no junkie. I'm not out here doing any and everything to get a hit. I just be chilling.

"Let me go." I stated calmly after he held me still for a few minutes. I needed to get the hell away from him and I was never going to talk to him again. I was beyond ashamed at the fact that he now knew about my habit.

"I can stop at any time." I reassured both him and myself. He didn't respond. I grabbed my purse and headed for the door.

"Arteal." Terrance called out. I stopped in my tracks but didn't turn around. "My mom is a junkie." he said with so much pain in his voice that I couldn't stop the tears from falling down my cheeks if I wanted to.

I could hear Terrance's shoes scrub against the hard, cheap carpet as he made his way towards me. I broke down further when he wrapped his arms around me in a gentle way. He walked me over to the bed, sat down then pulled me in the bed with him.

My clothes were drenched but Terrance didn't seem to mind as he rubbed his fingers through my hair.

Chapter 11

Zaria

The next morning, I woke up extremely nauseous. I groaned as I climbed out of bed and made my way to the bathroom. The door was locked and I sighed heavily with disappointment. I could feel it rising so I ran out of the front door then threw up in our yard.

My stomach began to cramp once I started to dry heave. "Fuck!" I said as I wiped my mouth with the back of my hand. I stood up and placed my hand on my stomach. It was hurting so bad but I guess this is something that I'm going to have to get used to.

I turned around and headed back for the door but the sight of my dad stopped me dead in my tracks. He stood in the doorway and just stared at me without saying a word. I wondered if he saw me throwing up but then I figured how could he not.

I ignored his look and ducked past him then ran straight to my room. I was a nervous wreck the next three days. So nervous in fact that I only came out to eat and use the bathroom. I hadn't answered any calls from Arteal, Damon or Kyle because I didn't want to talk to anyone or see anyone.

I laid across my bed trying to figure out what I was supposed to do with my life now. Here I am eighteen years old with a baby on the way and I still live at home with my parents. I could feel that familiar knot forming in my throat.

A knock at the door knocked me all the way out of my feelings. I sat up and didn't know what to think when I saw both of my parents at my door. My dad looked like he wanted to kill everybody and my mom looked like she had been crying. She walked in first.

"Baby we need to talk." She said and I got nervous instantly. I just stared at her and waited for her to tell me what it was that we needed to talk about because I didn't have anything to get off my chest. There was no way that I was about to tell them about this baby.

"Are you pregnant Zaria?" she asked and my mouth fell open. I wanted to answer her question with a lie but I felt like she already knew the truth. If I lied now she might hit me in the mouth or something. Although I'm eighteen I was still scared to tell my parents that I was pregnant.

I'd heard about how my dad was back in his day and how my mom was right there with him. I knew they would kill Damon if they found out he was my child's father because of the age difference. The last thing I needed was my dad locked up in jail because I'd gone out and got pregnant by someone his age.

I shook my head slowly but the look on my mom's face caused tears to fall down my eyes. "Yes ma'am." I said with a cracked voice.

"By who?" my dad asked as he stepped all the way in the room. "Kyle." I lied and shock filled both of their faces. My dad's facial expression quickly went from one of shock to one of anger then he stormed out of the room.

"Dad, wait!" I yelled but my mom stopped me with a shake of her head. "Let him cool off. We gotta go." She said then walked out of the room. I was confused but I knew better than to question anything at this point.

I got up and got dressed then headed out to the living room where my mom sat waiting on me. I still didn't ask her any questions because I didn't know how to. She hadn't snapped out yet about this pregnancy but I just knew that she would have by now.

About twenty minutes later we pulled up to the abortion clinic and I swear my heart jumped out of my chest. I looked between her and the building with my mouth open.

"Don't look at me like you stupid let's go. You walking round this bitch throwing up like we stupid. I knew before ya lil hoe ass graduated." She snapped as she got out of the car then closed the door behind her.

I rolled my eyes but I didn't dare budge. I know a couple of days ago I wasn't sure what I wanted but now that we sat outside of the clinic, I knew this wasn't what I wanted to do. I looked over at my mom as she stood in front of the car giving me attitude for days.

She had her hair pulled back into a tight ponytail and she wore a fitted white T shirt with skinny jeans and white sandals. She stood in front of the car with a deep frown etched on her dark skinned face, one hand on her hip and she used the other one to signal for me to get out of the car.

When I didn't move fast enough for her, she stormed to my side of the car. Tears began to fall at a rapid pace. I quickly hit the button to lock all of the car doors. She tilted her head to the side as if she couldn't believe I had done that.

"OPEN THIS DAMN DOOR BITCH!" she screamed as she slapped the window. I jumped hard as fuck and I think I pissed a little bit too. I shook my head as I crawled into the driver's seat. She ran around to the other side of the car like a maniac and banged on the window.

"GET OUT!" she screamed and hit the window again. I shook my head again as I cried. She nodded her head then dug through her purse until she came back up with the car keys. I crawled back over to the passenger's side.

She unlocked the door, opened it then reached over and grabbed my hair. She pulled me across the seat and out of the car as I tried to pry her hands from around my ponytail. "Mama stop please!" I begged as I cried out.

"That's what you should have told the lil nigga before he nutted in yo piss po' ass! Ain't got a pot to piss in or a window to throw it out of but you wanna have a baby!" she snapped as she dragged me to the door. "Now you walk in here like you got some sense." She said and let me go.

I followed her inside with my head held low. She guided me to a seat then walked up front to sign me in. About thirty minutes later, I was being called to the back. They gave me a pregnancy test and ultrasound. I was twelve weeks and three days pregnant.

The lady escorted me into another room where I was told to watch a video that would explain what was about to happen to my child. After the video was over, I was then escorted to another room then asked to strip down and place the gown on.

I cried the entire time that it took me to change into the gown and sit on the table. The person performing the abortion walked in with a strange look on his face then sat next to me.

"Are you sure you want to do this?" he asked and I shook my head because I didn't want to do this at all. I wanted to keep my baby even though I wasn't ready for it. I was sure I could learn how to be a parent if I was given the chance.

"You don't have to do this if you don't-"

I hopped down before he could even finish his sentence and began to put my clothes back on. My tears turned into tears of joy. I get to keep my baby and there's nothing my mom can do about it.

"You will not get a refund." He said and I nodded my head because I didn't give a fuck. All I cared about was being able to keep my child. I'm sure everything will work itself out from here. I thanked the man and headed back out into the waiting area in better spirits.

As soon as I made it in the waiting area my eyes connected with my mom's and I saw the rage behind them. She stood up and walked out of the door without a word. Fear gripped my soul as I stepped out of the door slowly.

I didn't see her at all so I stepped all the way out of the door. WHAM! She punched me on the side of the head so hard that I stumbled into the side of the building. "You want to go out and get pregnant and think I'm going to take care of it?" she asked as she hit me again.

She struck me over and over until I fell into a ball next to the building. People walked past us to go into the building but nobody intervened. I prayed that she would stop and what felt like hours but probably only a few minutes later she did.

"Come get ya shit out my house Zaria." She said then headed to her car. I stood to my feet slowly and watched as she threw my purse out of her car's window and pulled off. My own mom left me stranded at the abortion clinic all because I didn't kill my child.

Chapter 12

Kyle

"What's up baby boy?" my mom walked into the living room and asked. I knew she could tell that I had a lot of stuff on my mind. I'd just graduated high school so this was supposed to be a joyous moment. I should still be in bliss but I wasn't.

I shook my head and continued to stare at the TV. I had been trying to watch it all morning as I sat on the couch in the living room but I just couldn't focus. It had been a few days since I talked to Zaria and I was beyond worried about her.

Given her current circumstances, I didn't know if she was ignoring me because she'd decided to go back to Twan's punk ass uncle or if something was wrong with her. The very least she could do was be woman enough about whatever it was to tell me.

"Lies boy now talk." my mom said then took a seat on the coffee table directly in front of the couch that I was sitting on. I didn't want to put her in Zaria's business but I knew she wasn't going to let me make it because of the relationship that she and I have.

"Is this about the lil girl you told me about?" she asked and I nodded my head. I had been talking about Zaria for years but my mom would always tell me to focus on school and track so I could get a scholarship for college. She always said no woman would want a man that couldn't provide and a man that couldn't provide shouldn't want to be in a relationship.

We weren't well off, but I don't think anyone at our school had a family that didn't absolutely need either a scholarship or loans. Hell nobody could afford to pay those loans back so I opted for a scholarship that I definitely got.

"So what happened?" she asked. I took a deep breath and told her everything without leaving anything out. By the time that I was finished she sat in front of me with her mouth hanging wide open. I was nervous because I had no clue what she was about to say.

"Maybe you should leave her alone until she figures out what she wants. She may not be done with Damon." my mom said with an irritated expression on her face.

"Why are you looking like that?" I asked her.

"We all went to school together. Damon is a year or two younger than me but we were all in school together. It's sickening to me that he would do such a thing. She don't deserve that." she said and I shook my head because she really didn't.

Leaving her alone wasn't an option at this point though. We had already started something and I honestly just wanted to see where it could go. We've never had a serious conversation about life so I don't really know what her plans are now that we are adults but I can't just walk away.

The way I see it is if we don't work out, at least I'll know I tried. I mean as long as she isn't still messing with Damon then I don't see why we wouldn't work out. I'm a pretty good dude and I'll do anything I can to help her and her baby.

"Alright ma. I'm about to hit up Twan and go shoot some hoops at the park. Gotta work tomorrow so I'll be back early." I said to my mom to let her know the conversation was over. I needed to get out of the house and clear my head for a few hours. I pulled my phone out and called Twan.

"What's good Tyson?" he answered with a laugh. Him and his dad had been getting on me about jumping on Damon but if I could do it all over again, I'd do it the same damn way. Fuck all the dumb shit his old ass shouldn't have been picking up dates in the school zone.

"Man let's go to the park and shoot hoops." I said as I laughed at him. I knew this shit wasn't going to die down but I really didn't think the circumstances were funny at all. If I was Zaria's dad I'd kill him.

"Alright I'm bout to hit everybody up to meet us there." Twan said and hung the phone up. I walked to the back of the house and into my room so I could get dressed. I couldn't wait until August so I could get the hell out of dodge. I just hope Zaria comes with me.

Chapter 13

Zaria

I stood up and cried silently to myself as I hugged myself. I felt all alone. With nowhere to go, I grabbed my purse off the ground and started walking. I wandered into this little café just as a song started to play that caught my attention.

> "Crashing, hit a wall right now I need a miracle. Hurry up now I need a miracle.
> Stranded, reaching out I call your name but you're not around!
> I say your name but you're not around!
> I need you, I need you, I need you right now!
> Yea I need you right now!
> So don't let me, don't let me, don't let me down! I think I'm losing my mind now!
> It's in my head, darling I hope that you'll be here when I need you the most!
> So don't let me, don't let me, don't let me down! Don't let me down, down, down!
> Don't let me down, don't let me down, down, down.
> Don't let me down, Don't let me down, down, down.
> Running out of time I really thought you were on my side.
> But now there's nobody by my side.
> I need you, I need you, I need you right now!
> Yea I need you right now!
> So don't let me, don't let me, don't let me down. I think I'm losing my mind now.

It' in my head, darling I hope that you'll be here when I need you the most.
So don't let me, don't let me, don't let me down. Don't let me down."

Tears fell down my face as I stood right next to the door and listened to the song until it ended. I stared down at the ground the entire time because I could only imagine the way people were staring at me. They probably thought I was crazy right now. Especially since my mom left me all lumped up.

I hadn't looked in the mirror yet but those licks were sounding off and dazed me a little bit so I'm almost certain that I'm all lumped up. Yesterday I was just pregnant. Today I'm pregnant and homeless. I need Damon to handle his part now more than ever.

I made my way to the counter so I could ask them what song was playing. "Hey excuse me." I called out and the girl turned around with an attitude like I had done something to her. I rolled my eyes and waited for her to walk over to me.

"Yes?" she asked and it was like she had a chip on her shoulder about something but I had never seen her before a day in my life! "I just wanted to know what was the name of that song and who sang it." I matched her attitude with one of my own.

This bitch just turned around and walked away. A white girl approached the counter. "That was don't let me down by the chainsmokers." She answered and I gave her a head nod. "Thank you." I said then walked away. I stopped suddenly because I had to know what the issue was.

"Excuse me." I called out again. She gave me even more attitude as she made her way back over to the counter. "Chelsie just answered ya question." She said, clearly annoyed. "Do you know me?" I asked and she shook her head and tried to walk away.

I reached over the counter and grabbed her arm. "Well what's the problem?" I asked and she snatched away from me so hard that I almost lost my balance. "Bitch you took my man!" she snapped and a gasp immediately flew out of my open mouth.

I was beyond confused because I wasn't even in a relationship with anyone. "I think you have me mistaken." I explained because this had to be some type of misunderstanding. I began to wish I had just walked right back out of the door.

"Naw Zaria. You took Kyle." She said and I tilted my head in confusion. I didn't know that he had anything going on with anyone so that wasn't my fault. "Oh yea?" I asked then chuckled lightly. I didn't give her time to respond before I headed back out of the door. I didn't have time for that shit.

I headed back out of the door and texted Arteal to get her to meet me at the local park. I still wasn't ready to tell her what was wrong or what had happened. All I wanted to do was crash with her for a couple of days if she and her mom didn't mind.

She told me that she was already at the park so I headed in that direction. Man I got so many cat calls that I wanted to give them all my number just to keep my mind busy. The fact that my life is getting to be more and more complicated was enough reason for me to keep it moving.

When I walked into the park I sighed with disappointment to find that Arteal was there along with Twan, Kyle and a few of our other classmates. From the bottles on the ground, I could tell that they had been here for a while and that was fine, I just wished she would have told me first.

Kyle rushed to me because we hadn't talked in about three days and I'm sure he wanted to know why. I really didn't see a big deal in the whole situation because we never talked every day before this happened.

"What happened to you?" he asked with concern evident in his voice. He reached out to touch my face as he examined it but I snatched my face out of his hand. "Shouldn't you be worried about your girlfriend at the coffee shop?" I asked and shocked the hell out of him.

The shock was quickly replaced with anger. "She did this?" he asked as he began to breathe heavily and I shook my head. The truth is I only brought her up because I could barely stand to look at him right now because of my last encounter with Damon.

I knew I was going to have to choose and as good of a dude as Kyle is, he just can't do anything for me and my child. With me being homeless, I need Damon to get my spot for me now more than ever.

"I'm going to handle her." Kyle said but I shook my head. "Naw no need. I'm done." I said then walked past him and headed over to Arteal. I figured now is a better time than any to tell her what happened. I knew the truth is the only way she will take me back to her house right now.

Chapter 14

Arteal

I stared at Zaria as she stood in front of me at the table. She looked like she wanted to tell me something and from the looks of her appearance, I may need a bump to hear this story. I shook my head to rid myself of the thoughts because I'd promised Terrance that I wouldn't touch cocaine anymore. He was in so much pain from having to see his mom like that, that I didn't want him to be worried about me as well.

I hopped down off the table, grabbed Zaria's hand and led her away from everyone else to my car. We both climbed inside and shut the doors just to ensure that we had privacy.

"So who did that to you?" I asked as I rotated my body sideways to face her. She stared at me with a frown on her face then touched her nose softly. "Your nose is bleeding." she said as she continued to look at me.

I leaned over her and grabbed a few napkins out of the glove compartment. I stayed prepared when things like this happened because a nosebleed had become pretty normal for me.

"My mom." she finally answered the question once I was able to stop the bleeding. After she finished telling me what happened, I wanted to go to her house and give Tammy a piece of my mind.

Just because she killed all of her babies in high school doesn't mean that Zaria will want to kill all of hers. My mom told me all about how Dank use to get her and other chicks pregnant all the time and make them get abortions. She'd had so many that she was told she wouldn't be able to have children. Zaria was a miracle and that's why she's the only child.

She was the first child that her mom held long enough to have a live birth. Three failed attempts after Zaria has stopped them from trying again.

"I'm pissed Zaria but I know my mom won't care if you move in. We just have to find jobs to help out around the house." I said to her and she looked a bit uneasy. Shit you can't live with a mufucker for free so she might as well get used to working now that she's on her own.

"I was thinking about calling Damon to tell him I needed a place to stay."

I could have slapped fire out of her dumb ass when she said that. I looked over at Kyle who sat on the table and stared off into space as everyone around him laughed and talked. This isn't the Kyle I'm use to seeing and Zaria is going to fuck him up with this bullshit.

"Why would you want to do that? If you've never even been there before then why would you think he would let you move in?" I asked and she gave me a slight shoulder shrug. She hadn't thought this through at all.

"Listen, where is he now?" I asked as I cranked my car. I watched her check the time on her phone. It was almost eleven. "Work." she said. After she told me where he worked, we headed straight there.

I could tell she was nervous because she hadn't said a word the entire way there. When I pulled into the parking lot, I saw him walking out of the door. "Ah man he's about to take his break." Zaria said like we missed him. Shit the way I saw it is if he's about to take a break then he's free to talk.

I circled the building so I could park next to him but by the time I made it back around, he was leaving. I had to follow him because this is a conversation they needed to have in person.

"What are you doing?" Zaria asked with alarm evident in her voice. Shit you would have thought that I was trying to kill him the way she was acting. At least if he goes home, she will know where he lives so I'm actually doing her two favors.

"We're gonna see where he's going. Call him." I instructed. She looked hesitant at first, but she dialed his number and placed the call on speakerphone.

"How are my babies doing?" he cooed into the phone. It made me smile that he actually cared. When I looked over at Zaria, I could tell that she was happy about that as well. "He may not be too bad." I thought to myself as I continued to follow him.

"Doing well. What are you doing?" she asked as if she didn't already know.

"They worked me hard today baby. I'm mufucking tied!" he said with a laugh. Zaria joined in and glanced over at me. I just shook my head.

"Can you come see me on your break? We need to talk." Zaria asked.

"Baby I don't think I'm going to get a break today but I'll call you when I get off. My boss just walked into my office." he lied smoothly as he turned into an exquisite neighborhood. It was so nice that I didn't even know that it existed before now.

"Alright." she sighed into the phone. I could tell she was completely disappointed and it wasn't just a front for him. She ended the call and sat in her seat looking straight ahead. She looked calm but the fact that her leg was shaking let me know how mad she really was.

"Listen, when we pull up, play it cool. Don't go in because you don't know what you are walking in on." I explained to her. I knew she didn't want to hear it but I was saving her more pain.

Damon ended up parking in front of the most beautiful house I had ever seen. All I could think about was how he told Zaria she couldn't come over because it was a bad area. This is by far the best area to come over to.

Chapter 15

Damon

I hated to lie to Zaria like that because I do care about her. Now that she's the mother of my child, I care about her a little bit more. I just don't love her. I'll probably never love her because I can't honestly say that I love myself.

My whole life it'd been a battle within. I knew exactly what I wanted and I was raised to think it was wrong. Now don't get me wrong, I'm all man.

There's nothing feminine about me. I'm just a man that loves men.

I'm not going to pretend like somebody molested me because that wasn't the case. Nobody ever touched me, well, not in that way. My mama used to tear me out of the frame when I would try to tell her how I felt. It was like she thought that she could beat the gay out of me.

Before Zaria, I had never been interested in any woman. That's how I knew she was something special. Someone I needed to hold on to. That's why even now as I pulled into Bae's driveway, I knew I couldn't let her go.

I shut the engine off then made my way to the door. He always kept it unlocked for me so I didn't have to hang around outside each day and wait for him to come and answer it. I opened the door and made my way inside.

I took my shoes off at the door then closed it shut. His wife had this thing about people walking through her house with their shoes on. I don't understand it.

Now that I think about it, I don't understand our situation at all. Here I am in love with a man that I can't go public with because for one, he's married and second of all he's on the down low. Meanwhile there's this young lady that loves me and everything that she knows about me and I'm treating her the same way that James is treating me.

Yet here I am, making my way towards the master bedroom so I could make love to my man in the bed that he probably makes love to his wife in. I made my way slowly because I was here for more than just that reason alone. I needed to tell him about Zaria and I's baby.

"I've been missing you." James said as soon as I made my way into the room. For the first time in years, I stared at the man that I loved and didn't get that feeling that I normally get from looking at his naked, chocolate, muscular frame against their cream colored sheets.

I finally knew how Zaria felt the day she walked away from me in her backyard. The only difference is, I knew I should have been done but I wasn't as strong as Zaria when it came to this type of shit because I didn't want to hurt anyone.

"We need to talk." I said as I sat on the edge of the bed. He sighed dramatically because he thought this was about to be another "leave your wife" conversation but I was done with those. Shit I was at the point where I was willing to take whatever I could get.

"What's up now?" he asked and I could tell he was aggravated already. I knew what he wanted me to do to him and talk to him wasn't on the list. Plus I only got an hour for lunch and he knew I'd have to get back to work soon.

"So I started seeing someone else a few months ago." I began.

James crawled over to me seductively and removed my shirt. "Do he kiss and lick your ear like this?" he asked as he slipped his warm, wet tongue in my ear. That was my spot and he already knew that.

I could feel my dick get hard as his kisses trailed down my neck. "Do he make you feel like this?" he asked as he made his way down my chest. I moaned out softly.

"We can talk later. We don't have time now." James said as he laid under the covers on his stomach with his ass slightly raised for me. I shook my head because he was right but I wasn't feeling this at the moment.

All I could think about was Zaria as I reached in his underwear draw and grabbed the lube from underneath all of his underwear and socks. I squirted some in the palm of my hands and applied it to my hard dick.

I climbed on the bed and rubbed some of it on and around his asshole. I removed the cover just enough to pull it around me as I began to spread his cheeks. He moaned in anticipation of what was to come.

I slid in slowly but everything felt different now. I'd grown used to Zaria's pussy gripping my dick as I slid in and out of her at a rapid pace. James moaned out, but I was in another world. A world with just Zaria and I.

Chapter 16

Zaria

Arteal tried her best to talk me out of going in the house to confront Damon and even tried to drive off before I could get out of the car but I wasn't having that. There was no way that I was going to be the only one hurt in this situation.

Damon needed to know that I knew where he lived and that he had lied about everything. He didn't let me come to his home because he shared it with someone else. The car that he pulled next to proved that to me!

I was beyond pissed as I made my way to the door. I wanted to bang on the door and cause a scene for all of their uppity ass neighbors to see but I decided to just surprise the fuck out of both of them and see if the door was unlocked.

The first thing I saw was a pair of Damon's shoes behind the door. All of the other shoes I didn't recognize. I sucked my teeth then shook my head. Naw I wasn't here to be courteous. I was here to let shit be known. I walked towards the back of the house with my flip flops on and prayed every step of the way that I at least smudged some dirt on their khaki carpet.

I could hear soft moans and to be honest, my heart jumped into my throat. I slowed my pace and began to have second thoughts. I could hear Damon's deep moans so she must have been rocking his world because I'd never been able to make him moan like that.

The tears fell down my face rapidly as I cried softly. I lost my balance and fell against the wall and made a loud thud. I could hear shuffling on the other side of the door. I'd lost my nerve to do this completely.

I jumped up and ran back out of the door. I couldn't confront anyone crying the way I was crying. I didn't want anyone to know that I was hurting.

"What happened?" Arteal stepped out of the car and asked with a deep frown on her face.

"Get back in the car!" I yelled with tears still streaming down my face as I ran around the side of the car and hopped in. Arteal followed suit with a questioning look on her face.

"JUST GO!" I yelled just as I saw the door open from the corner of my eye. I glanced over just in time to see Damon standing in the doorway wearing only his boxers. His mouth hung open in disbelief.

My eyes didn't leave his until I could no longer see him. The tears just kept pouring from my eyes. I tried desperately to stop them but nothing worked. Every time that I wiped a tear off, it was replaced with three more.

"Zaria I-"

"Don't"

I cut her off because I didn't want to hear anything. All I wanted to do was go home and hide under my covers. The only problem with that is I didn't have a home to go to. My parents had kicked me out when I refused to get an abortion. I had nowhere to go and I didn't know what to do.

It felt like my life was over. A sharp pain went through my stomach as it began to cramp. I cried hard and balled my body up in pain.

"Zaria, are you ok?" Arteal asked as she swerved the car slightly. She regained control of the car as I continued to cry out in pain. "My stomach." I managed to force out. It felt like something was balling my stomach up in knots and I couldn't take it.

Arteal grabbed her phone and placed a call. "I'm taking you to the hospital." She said as she placed the phone to her ear. I guess they didn't answer her because she had to call right back.

"No disrespect but don't yell at me!" she snapped and I wondered who she was talking to. All I wanted her to do was get me some help.

"I'm on my way to the hospital with your daughter! Meet us there she may be having a miscarriage!" she snapped again.

"Noooo!" I cried out at the thought of losing my child. I had literally just found out that I was pregnant so I couldn't be about to lose it already. This can't be life right now. There's no way that I could be about to go through this without Damon.

Zaria: think im having a miscarriage

Damon: where are you

Zaria: ER

Another sharp pain shot through my stomach just as Arteal whipped the car into the parking lot. By this time, she'd already hung the phone up. I could tell that she was worried about me by the look on her face as she pulled under the pavilion.

She hopped out of the car to get help. They ran out the door with her with a wheelchair and helped me get in then wheeled me straight to the back. I wanted Arteal to stay with me but I knew she had to go move the car. I felt so alone.

Damon: OMW

I was able to catch a glimpse of the text before the nurse pulled the phone out of my hand. She raised the sleeve on my shirt and applied the blood pressure cuff. Once she finished checking my vital signs she left out of the room just as quickly as she had come.

"Good evening, I'm Doctor Avery, what seems to be the problem?" she asked with a pleasant smile on her face. Her smile alone made me a little bit comfortable as I began to describe the pain I felt. She didn't look the least bit worried as she placed a reassuring hand on my shoulder.

"It could be stress. Calm down for me while I get the ultrasound tech in here so we can check on the little one." She said as she gestured towards my stomach. I nodded my head and she left the room.

I sighed heavily after about fifteen minutes had passed and I still laid in the hospital bed alone.

The ultrasound technician hadn't come into my room yet and neither had Arteal. I didn't want to go through this alone so I pressed the call button so I could get them to bring someone in with me.

"May I help you?" a voice answered the call button.

"Is there someone out front for me? I don't want to be alone." I stated. My voice cracked as I spoke so I already knew that she could hear the nervousness in my voice.

"Alright I'll send them back." She said and I smiled to myself because that meant Damon was here. As mad as I am at him right now I needed him here with me more than ever. I didn't have this baby alone so I shouldn't be back here going through this alone.

A few minutes later Arteal walked in with one hell of an attitude followed by my mom who had one as well. I know them both so I can tell that they've had an exchange of words and by the looks of things, those weren't very pleasant words.

My mom didn't say a thing to me. She simply sat in the chair next to the bed and crossed her arms over her chest. Arteal noticed it too and rolled her eyes then grabbed the chair next to hers and pulled it away from her before she sat down.

"What have they said so far?" Arteal asked.

"Could be stress. I'm waiting on the ultrasound tech." I said.

As if right on cue, in walks the ultrasound tech ready to check on my baby.

Chapter 17

Damon

I didn't know how much Zaria saw when she came into James' house. Hell I wasn't aware that she was even following me. The only reason I jumped out of the bed before James is because I know how his wife Teresa would have acted had she'd been the one to hear moaning in her house.

Well I take it back, I didn't know who it was, I just knew it wasn't Teresa. When I hopped out of the bed I caught a glimpse of her as she turned the corner to run out of the door. I tried to stop her so I could explain but I couldn't. Now because of all this shit I could be about to lose my child.

James had been calling me back to back since I ran out on him. I ignored every call though and even called in to work to let my manager know that a family emergency had arisen. Since I'd never done that before, he understood and let me off the rest of the day.

I ran into the emergency room and straight up to the front desk. I gave the front desk clerk Zaria's name and almost slapped her when she called someone and told them her dad was out front. I know I'm old enough to be her father but damn the little rude bitch didn't have to assume that I was. Like a man my age and a woman of Zaria's age dating is uncommon.

She gave me her room number and opened the doors for me so I rushed on to the back. As I turned on the hall that her room is located on, I noticed a lady about to push a machine inside of the room. I didn't want to miss any part of this.

"Wait!" I yelled out to stop her. I could tell she was about to say something to Zaria by the way her mouth was still parted when she turned to look in my direction.

"May I help you?" she asked as she placed her hand on her hip.

"I'm the father." I said and her mouth dropped. I could tell she wasn't expecting that but oh fucking well. I didn't have time for shit like this. All I had time for was making sure my child is straight.

I walked into the room and came face to face with my classmate Rita. She jumped to her feet and looked between Zaria and I a few times.

"Aw shit." Zaria's friend said as she began to scoot her chair out of the way.

"The father?" she asked with her eyebrows raised slightly as she continued to look between us. I nodded my head and glanced over at Zaria. She laid on the bed with a pained expression on her face.

"Yes but now isn't the time to- "

"The hell it isn't! Nigga you damn near forty and you been fucking my baby?!" she screamed out. The lady with the machine gasped loudly then she scurried off more than likely to get security.

"What happened, happened Rita damn can't take it back now." I stated plainly with a shrug.

"You two know each other? How?" Zaria asked.

"I thought you said this was Kyle's child?" Rita asked through squinted eyes.

"Oh yea? You been fucking both of us?" I asked because that shit really hurt to hear.

"Didn't I just walk in on you fucking your wife?!" Zaria snapped as tears rolled down her eyes. I gave her a confused expression before I responded.

"I'm not married." I said with a sigh of relief. She hadn't seen anything; she'd only heard James' moans. Shit I almost smiled because now I know this shit is fixable.

"Do we have a problem here?" a security guard asked from the door. I said no but Rita said yes and I could tell that it threw the officer off a little bit.

"This is my daughter and I want him out."

"I wasn't your daughter when you beat me up and put me out."

"Sir, I'm eighteen. I want my mom out." Zaria said and there wasn't a jaw that wasn't on the floor after that. I looked over at Rita and could see that she was extremely hurt by what had just taken place.

Rita stared at Zaria for several seconds before she walked out of the room and made sure she bumped me on the way out. I know now that Zaria and I are going to have to have a talk if Rita is still with that nigga Dank.

Chapter 18

Arteal

\

I absolutely could not believe that Zaria chose this man over her own mom. I know they had gotten into it earlier today but I mean damn! She had literally just caught this mufucker with someone else. But how quick did she forgive when his ass said he wasn't married.

Ok so what, he's not married! He was still fucking somebody in that big pretty nice ass house.

His phone started to ring and I watched him pull it out to silence it before he waved the ultrasound tech inside of the room.

She asked us to step outside because she had to make room for the machine. It was perfectly fine though because we heard that strong heartbeat from outside of the door. I smiled as I watched the tears roll down Zaria's cheek. I just wished Ms. Rita was able to witness this moment. Maybe she would have allowed Zaria to come home.

Once the girl finished, she moved the machine out of the room and left. I walked in and sat down but all of a sudden the only thing I could think about was getting a bump. It hadn't been a whole twenty four hours yet since I told Terrance I would stop.

I told him I didn't need rehab or anything like that because I wasn't addicted to it I just enjoyed it. I really didn't know what to do at the moment but I knew I couldn't leave Zaria. I didn't know if she needed a ride or where Damon would take her.

"Are you ok?" Zaria asked with a frown on her face. I nodded quickly with a smile as Damon looked over at me suspiciously. It made me feel like he knew what was wrong as he stared at me.

"You sure?" Zaria asked with her hand on her stomach. "Are you still hurting?" I asked to get the attention off of me. My leg began to shake but I had no control of it so I stood up.

"Can I talk to her for a moment?" Zaria asked Damon. I sighed heavily and began to pace the floor. "Zaria I'm fine." I said but she just looked at Damon. I could tell that he didn't want to leave by the frown on his face.

His phone chimed. When he pulled the phone out of his pocket, he stormed out of the room without a word to anyone. Zaria looked confused but I knew that was the woman Zaria had heard him fucking. Someone had called him a lot since he'd been here anyway.

"So talk to me." Zaria said just as a nurse came in with a syringe to administer a low dose of pain medicine. She explained that it would not harm the baby at all and it was often used for nausea. After she left the room, Zaria stared at me.

"Close the door Arteal." She said from her position on the bed. I walked over and closed the door. I didn't want to tell her what was going on because I didn't want to hear anything about it. I'd been dealing with this so long alone that I wasn't ready to let anyone in.

"Talk to me." Zaria said and I shook my head. I could feel that oh so familiar lump form in my throat as all of the memories of my dad coming into my room flooded my brain at once. I stared down at the ground as I thought about everything and everyone I had done just to feel like I was in control. The tears burned my cheeks as I thought about how I had started to use drugs and how at that very moment, I wanted nothing more than a bump.

When I looked up at Zaria, tears were streaming down her cheeks as she watched me. She was already going through so much and I just didn't want any of my problems to add on to the fact that she's pregnant by someone else's man and homeless.

The last thing that she needs to worry about is her junkie best friend that does cocaine and will fuck anyone that can make her cum because her father molested her.

"I'm Zaria fine but I have to go." I said.

"NO!" she began. "When you hurt I hurt! Let me help you!" she cried out as she looked at me with pleading eyes. I took a seat next to her and told her about my dad. When I looked back up at her, I could see that she didn't know what to say. I mean who would?

"I gotta go." I said because I was embarrassed. I hated to leave her alone but I didn't want to go through the whole twenty one questions routine. Talking about it wouldn't help me.

When I made it out into the lobby I broke down crying. Crazy thing is, it was filled with people waiting to be seen by a doctor. I continued to leave as I wiped the tears from my eyes.

I climbed in my car and made my way to the nearest hood so I could do what I needed to do to get a bump. I pulled up into unknown territory, parked my car then got out and made my way up to the first corner boy I saw.

"Hey um got snow?" I asked and he looked at me crazy.

"Get from round here." He said as he looked over his shoulder. I looked with him because I didn't know what he was looking for. I was here now so I wasn't going to leave until I got what I'd come here to get.

“Listen, I just need a little bit.” I pleaded. “I don’t have any money but I’ll do anything.” I continued and his eyes lit up. He looked back again then jogged off in the direction of another guy. When he returned, he held up the little baggie and I almost jumped for joy.

“Let’s go.” He said as he grabbed my arm and pulled me on the side of the house. As soon as we were out of view, he unbuckled his pants and pulled his dick through the slit. I suddenly got cold feet.

I mean I’d sucked plenty of dicks before but never had I gone this far to do it in exchange for a drug I shouldn’t even be using. I dropped down to my knees and pulled his semi hard dick into my mouth.

His nuts smelled sweaty, kind of like must and old ground beef. My eyes watered as he forced himself all the way in my mouth. I gagged and tried to pull back but he placed his hands firmly around the back of my head and rammed himself all the way back in.

Tears flowed from my eyes as I tried to hold my breath so I could no longer smell him. Several minutes passed before he let up. I immediately threw up all over the ground right next to him. He tossed the baggie on my lap as I sat on the ground and tried to get myself together enough to head on home.

I wiped my mouth with the back of my hand and stood to my feet with the baggie in my hand. I damn near ran to my car to get the hell away from these people. As soon as I made it to the car, I pulled off only to pull over on the side of the road because I became too emotional to drive.

I cried as I sprinkled some peace on the area between my thumb and index. I knew I needed help at this point but I wasn't going to get it. I needed this hit more than anything. I reasoned that I was a much better person with this.

I snorted it all then laid my head back and welcomed my peace only seconds later. The tears no longer fell and my mind was finally clear. This drug helped me. It has become my peace and now I knew what to do to help Zaria get hers.

I drove back to the house we followed Damon to and this time there was another car parked next to the car that he parked next to earlier. I shook my head at how he's played my girl all of this time. I walked over to the new car to see which one needed the note.

Once I noticed a tube of lipstick and an ID badge with a beautiful woman pictured on it I shook my head. “Sorry Teresa but Zaria can’t be the only one hurting here.” I said out loud to myself as I ran back to my car.

I wanted to go back to tell Zaria what I was thinking but I knew she wouldn’t approve of it. I needed to set something up so all of them would know everything. It was the only way for Zaria to get proof.

I hopped back in my car and zoomed to the library because it was the only place with a meeting room that was completely free. All you needed was a library card and I kept mine in my car. Once I pulled up to the library, I hopped out.. a woman on a mission.

Chapter 19

Kyle

I headed home completely worried about Zaria. If I could take her pain away I will. All she has to do is give me a chance and I know I can make her happy. I didn't have a father figure but I know to just treat her how I want someone to treat my mom.

I kind of wanted to stop by the coffee shop to handle that issue but knowing her, she'll deny it then come at Zaria harder next time she sees her so I decided to leave that alone.

I bypassed my mom and headed straight to the bathroom to hop in the shower. Once I finished, I walked in the living room just as my phone started ringing. I walked over to it and a look of confusion crossed my face as I answered.

"Hello?" I answered.

"Hey um Kyle, are you busy? This is Zaria." She spoke hesitantly. I could tell she needed me and she needed to know that I'd do anything for her.

"No. Why are you at the hospital?" I asked as I headed back to my room to put my shoes on. She wouldn't have called if she didn't need me to come to her. My mom cut her eyes at me but didn't say a word. I ignored her silent warning and kept moving.

"A little discomfort but I'm ok now." She said softly.

Silence.

"I'm on my way, Zaria." I said and heard her sigh into the receiver. "Thank you." She said and I ended the call. She didn't need to thank me because I was only doing what I would want someone to do for my mom.

She trusted me enough to call me so she had to have known that I would indeed come through for her. I put my shoes on and walked back through the house to go outside.

"Kyle." My mom called out.

When I turned around to look at her she had a worried look on her face. She knew everything about this situation so I knew she was worried about me putting too much into her while she put too much into someone else.

"Be careful." She said and I nodded my head and left the house. I didn't know if Zaria needed a ride from the emergency room or what but I needed to get to her fast. Once I got there, I parked and headed straight to the front desk clerk and gave her Zaria's name.

"You must be the daddy?" she assumed. "Go on back to room 18." She said with a smile. I smiled back and made my way through the double doors to check on Zaria.

When I walked in her room, she had dried up tears on cheeks but she smiled at me when she noticed me. "Thanks for coming." She said and I gave her a head nod as I made my way to the sink.

I grabbed two paper towels and wet one of them then approached her bedside and wiped her face clean. Then I used the dry paper towel to dry it off. She laid on the bed fully dressed and I didn't know if she had just gotten here or if she was about to be discharged.

A few seconds later, a nurse walked in and handed her her discharge papers. “Take it easy Ms. Jones.” She called Zaria by her last name. Zaria nodded her head and climbed out of bed.

“You don’t need a wheelchair?” I asked and she laughed as she shook her head at me. I slid my arm around her lower back and led her out of the room and passed the nurse that had just walked out of the room. She smiled at us, probably assuming that I was the child’s father like the girl upfront.

I helped her get in the front seat of my car and ran around to the driver’s side and pulled off. I just rode around and let her listen to the radio. I waited on her to tell me where she needed me to take her to but she never did. I waited for her to tell me what was on her mind but she didn’t do that either.

“Are you hungry?” I asked and she nodded her head. I drove straight to Applebee’s so we could sit down and both get full while enjoying each other’s company for twenty dollars. She smiled as we walked hand in hand into the restaurant.

She smiled the whole time as we ate and joked around like we used to in school. I never wanted that smile to go away but by the time we left Applebee’s it had gotten late and I still didn’t know where to take her.

"Are you going home?" I asked as we got back into the car. I glanced over at her and watched the happiness leave her face as her eyes glistened with tears.

"Talk to me." I said to her as she looked down. She said something but I didn't hear what she said.

"I don't have anywhere to go." She said a bit louder. My heart literally went out to her. I nodded my head and drove straight to best western. I hadn't spent a dime of my money in the two years that I'd been working because my mom wanted me to save it for an emergency. She still paid my phone bill and all of the things I needed she bought it for me.

I parked the car, got out and went inside. I figured since she didn't have anywhere to go I'd just pay for her a room for the rest of the week and we'd figure out what to do after that when the time came.

I helped her up to her room and she cried silently the whole time. I figured she was just happy that she wouldn't have to worry for a while.

Chapter 20

Zaria

I was beyond thankful for Kyle getting me this room but by the third day, I felt like I was in prison! I didn't have transportation and Kyle worked the next couple of days. He told me that he picked a few extra shifts so he had been working double shifts all day. I was so lonely and Damon hadn't talked to me since he left the hospital.

I had no idea what his problem was but I grew more and more frustrated with each call that he sent to voicemail. This wasn't right at all! For months he had been promising me that we'd move in together and now that I needed him, I was forced to depend on someone else.

I'd reached out to my parents but they weren't taking my calls either so the only people I had talked to were Kyle and Arteal. She was up to something, but I hadn't figured out what it was yet. She was being really secretive and when she came by yesterday, she was really jumpy.

"Ugh!" I sighed in utter frustration when Damon sent me to voicemail again. I just didn't understand what was going on. I began to think about how often we talked in the beginning, but they must have been having problems or something.

I shook my head just as there was a knock on my door. I swung it open just to come face to face with Arteal. She doesn't really look like herself anymore these days. She'd been losing a considerable amount of weight but she wouldn't tell me what was wrong with her.

I stepped to the side and allowed her to come in. She was all over the place saying all kinds of things but nothing at all. I just looked at her because I had no idea what party she was talking about. Plus the last thing I wanted to do was party.

"Girl c'mon and get dressed we can get wasted!" she yelled excitedly.

"What the fuck are you high or something because I'm pregnant!" I said and watched her eyes get big. I replayed what I had just said to her in my head to figure out what I said that was offensive. Nothing registered.

"I'm not high! I just want to have fun." She lied. I only knew she was lying because she began to play with her fingers and look down to the ground. She could never make eye contact when she lied about anything either.

I took in her appearance again as my eyes welled up with tears. Her clothes were baggy and wrinkled. Her cheekbones were sunken in and I could see her collarbone. My best friend had been battling a demon and I had paid no attention to her. It's bad enough that she'd been molested and I had no idea about that either.

I grabbed her around the shoulders and forced her to take a seat. She was not going to be able to run out this time.

"What is wrong with you?" I asked and she began to fidget nervously. "Nothing Zaria, I just want to get out and enjoy myself with my best friend. Please don't make this about me when you're the one that's been holed up in this hotel room." She said as she stood back up.

I nodded my head and took a step backwards. "Well ok but I'm wearing this." I said with a slight shrug of my shoulders. She smiled then jumped up, grabbed my hand and pulled me out of the hotel.

We rode around for about fifteen minutes before we pulled up at the library. I looked at her crazy because we never hung out at the library when we were in school so she better know I don't want to hang out at the library now that we are out of school.

"Why are we here?" I asked and a slow smile spread across her face.

"It's a surprise!" she said as he climbed out of the car then raced around to my side. I climbed out of the car so she wouldn't try to pull me out of it.

We walked arm in arm through the parking lot when I spotted Damon's car. "Is this my baby shower?" I asked completely excited once I saw Damon's car. It explained why he hadn't been answering any of my calls.

He had been so busy helping Arteal with this baby shower. Then it hit me. "Wait, we don't know what I'm having." I said and Arteal gave me a strange look. Normally I can read her like a book but I was having the hardest time figuring out what was going on.

Chapter 21

Arteal

2 days ago…..

"What kind of invitations are you looking for?" the store clerk asked me. Shoot I was still trying to figure out what kind of party this was going to be. All I knew so far was that I was going to expose Damon to his precious wife Teresa.

I'd already looked through her car and found out where she worked. They both left their cars unlocked but didn't keep cash in them. When I searched the other car I found a credit card that had Teresa Smith on it.

Smith is also my last name but it's a common name. I just hope she isn't like a distant cousin or something like that. I'd hope I wouldn't have to set up a family member the way I was about to set her up.

"Just a casual invitation. It's a surprise party." I finally answered the store clerk. I was about to use Teresa's credit card to send her a bouquet of pink roses along with a card telling her to meet her lover at the library at seven at night. The library closed at eight so I had her scheduled to walk in right before us.

Once I paid for the transaction, I drove to another flower shop and purchased two more bouquets of roses. I wanted to be sure that Damon got his so I sent them to him at his job and at his home. I was not about to play any games with these people about Zaria.

Present day…..

"Uh… girl it doesn't matter. Everybody knows to get neutral colors." I lied because I didn't want her to want to leave. We were here now so there was really no point in turning back now. I couldn't believe that I was about to do this.

The closer we got to the doors the more amped up I got about the whole situation. This is what needed to be done and I knew Zaria wasn't bold enough to do it. I'd covered all bases and wrote his wife a note just to let her know that her husband had another woman pregnant but she'd probably just write it off once she sees the roses.

"My parents. Are they coming?" Zaria asked and I had to shake my head. This wasn't that kind of party hell. We could have the baby shower when we actually found out what she was having. It'd be ridiculous to have one now.

"Don't worry c'mon." I said and grabbed her hand but she snatched away from me. I turned around to look at her and she had a disgusted look on her face. "Why are your hands so sweaty?" she frowned as she wiped her hand on her pants leg.

"Nervous I guess." I said with a slight shrug of the shoulder. Truth be told I was coming down off my high and needed another hit.

I'd gotten ridiculous and I knew I had begun to spiral out of control. I had been doing any and everything to that funky nut drug dealer to get more blow and it showed. I no longer recognized myself when I looked in the mirror so I stopped looking.

My mom asked me if I was on drugs and when I told her that I wasn't she just walked away. She hadn't hit me at all since she caught Terrance in the house but now she doesn't talk to me either. Although I'd thought about using stuff in the house to get money I didn't because I was more afraid of what she would do to me.

"After this we need to talk and you are going to tell me everything." Zaria said with a frown on her face. I nodded my head and she walked ahead of me. I don't know why she walked away so fast but I knew she had an attitude.

I did a light jog to catch up to her so I could lead her into the meeting room. See Zaria is one of those people that have to be pushed to do something. She won't just walk up to anyone and start anything but if it's brought to her she can handle herself. That's why I brought this to her.

I opened the door to the meeting room and their sat Damon. Alone. I began to get nervous because his wife should be here by now. They were supposed to be in here together when Zaria and I walked in.

"Aw fuck!" I said as I took a step backwards. My voice caught Damon's attention and he looked up at us with a confused look on his face. I'm sure he thought he was here to meet his wife or girlfriend whatever he calls her but that wasn't the case.

"What's going on? Zaria what uh, what um are you doing here?" Damon asked Zaria. She had stepped completely in the room with a smile on her face but now she looked just as confused as Damon did.

She turned around and looked at me with a questioning look. I needed a bump bad! “I’ll explain everything after I piss.” I rushed out then turned around and ran to the bathroom.

I splashed water on my face as I tried to figure out if this was the right approach to take to put everything out on the table. “It’s too late to turn back now.” I said as I used a napkin to shape my line of blow across the counter.

I leaned over and snorted it all up and felt that familiar state of bliss. I washed my face again and made sure there was no residue on my nose before I made my way back into the meeting room.

Chapter 22

Zaria

I was so confused but I think I know what Arteal was trying to do when she had Damon and I meet up here like this. I smiled at her for trying to make me happy but she went about it the wrong way. I'd love to be with Damon but I don't want to force anything.

"She told me this was for the baby shower." I said with a smile as I looked over at Damon's confused face.

"Baby shower? Who's pregnant?" A female asked as soon as she walked into the room. I jumped around in my seat as the reality of what Arteal was really up to set in. I thought this meeting was to get Damon and I back on good terms since he hadn't been speaking to me. The reality of the situation is that she wanted his wife to find out about me.

I shot daggers into the woman with my eyes for getting everything from Damon that I wanted. Oh how I wanted to tell her that I was pregnant by her man so she could feel the pain that I felt as I looked at her. My mouth hung open with everything that I wanted to say on the tip of my tongue but nothing came out.

“Teresa, what are you doing here?” Damon stood up and asked. He completely ignored her question.

“That’s what I’m trying to figure out.” she responded as she stared me up and down like I was the one in the wrong. If she wants to be mad at somebody she needs to be mad at Damon. That’s what’s wrong with females now! They always want to get mad at the other woman like she put a gun to her husband’s head.

“I’m fina get out of here.”

“Oh no you don’t!” I began as I gave Damon a hard enough shove to send him back down into his chair. “We’re all here now so we might as well get this show on the road.” I said then turned my attention back to Teresa.

Arteal walked back in the room looking happy and sweaty. I shook my head as she made her way over to me. My best friend is on drugs and I can look at her and tell that she’s not ok. I began to wonder how long she’d been on them and how far off track she is.

“Who’s the junkie?” Teresa asked with a slight smirk on her face.

“Bitch I’m no junkie! Don’t worry about me! What you need to be worried about is ya husband and why he got her pregnant!” Arteal yelled, acting all animated. I was so distracted by how she flailed her arms all over the place and bounced around as she yelled that I didn’t see Teresa charge at me until we both flipped over the table and landed on the floor on the other side.

“You like fucking people’s husband bitch?!” Teresa yelled as she sat on my chest and punched me in the face. I tried to get her off of me but she had too much power. I tried to swing at her but it was safer to use my arms to block her from hitting me in the face.

Arteal growled and dove over the table and knocked Teresa off of me. They went blow for blow as they rolled over each other. Damon ran around and helped me to my feet.

“Are you ok?” he asked as he placed his hand on my stomach in a loving way. Tears streamed down my face but not from any physical pain. Physically I was fine. My heart was broken though. I tried to cry out every drop of love that I had for this man as he caressed my face gently.

“You’re married.” I stated, but he shook his head and wiped my tears away. “If I was married I wouldn’t do this.” he said then kissed me softly and passionately. I tuned out the tussling that was going on between Arteal and Teresa as I returned the kiss.

“WHAT’S GOING ON?!” a deep voice boomed off the wall. Damon snatched completely away from me then backpedaled to get some distance between us. I stared at him with a confused look on my face. He looked like a deer caught in headlights.

Chapter 23

Arteal

This old bitch had them hands and was seriously giving me a run for my money. I stopped fighting her when I thought I heard someone kiss. I glanced over and couldn't believe my eyes as I watched Damon and Zaria kiss like we weren't on the ground five steps away from them fighting.

BAM!

Teresa hit me so hard that my head hit the floor and I was dazed momentarily. "Stupid bitches." I heard her mumble as she stood to her feet.

"WHAT'S GOING ON?"

My heart stopped beating and I think I died a little. I raised my hand and pinched myself just to make sure I was still here and that I wasn't dreaming. I sat up slowly with blood trickling down my nose.

"What's going on is your little bitch set up this little meeting with her junkie ass friend to tell me that she's pregnant!" I heard Teresa snap. She stood only a few steps away but her voice sounded like it was far away.

"Oh my God Arteal!" Zaria screamed at me. I glanced over at her and expected to see an angry expression on her face but it was one of worry. I followed her line of vision down to my pants. I hadn't even realized that I had pissed on myself.

"Oh great!" Teresa said as she threw her hands up in frustration.

"Arteal, say something." Zaria said as my body began to tremble. I raised a trembling hand and pointed at him. He looked at me like he had seen a ghost. When I called this meeting to expose everyone, I didn't think the pot of exposure would trickle over to me.

"My, my, my dad."

"Yo daddy?!" Teresa yelled as she ran over to him and started fighting him too. I just stood there trembling with my hand extended as I watched her send blow after blow to the man that ruined me, face.

Damon rushed over, grabbed Teresa by her shoulders and pulled her away from him. She bucked her body against Damon's in an attempt to break free so she could do more damage but he wouldn't let her go.

My eyes shot back to my dad, James Smith and he was already staring at me. "I'm sorry." he mouthed and tears started to flow nonstop.

Chapter 24

Zaria

Nothing made sense as I watched what was going on around me. I didn't know Arteal's dad was still alive. All she told me about him was that he'd touched her a few times when she was growing up. I didn't respond to her because I thought she was going to tell me more but instead she ran out of the room.

I watched how fast Damon rushed over to grab who I now know is Arteal's dad's wife off of him. My mind flashed back to the moment I entered the house and saw shoes near the door. I thought about all the shoes that were there and I only knew one pair for sure was Damon's.

I thought about the deep moans I heard as I made my way down the hallway. I knew I'd never made Damon sound like that, but I now know that it wasn't because she made him feel better. It was because it wasn't Damon that was moaning.

I thought about how Damon ran to the door to stop me but he didn't say anything once he got there. He couldn't say anything because the house I'd come in wasn't his house at all. The house belonged to Teresa and her husband.

I thought about how loving Damon just was only seconds before Arteal's dad made his presence known. After that, Damon got completely away from me. I thought he was caught off guard and didn't want anyone to see us since we had never been in public before but it wasn't people that he didn't want to see us. It was the man that had just walked in that he didn't want to.

"How could you do this to me James?" Teresa cried out. James rushed to her side just as she dropped down to her knees on the floor. He wrapped his arms around her tightly as she cried out.

"You have a daughter!" she cried and I watched with tears streaming down my cheeks. I looked up at Damon and he had a scowl on his face as he watched the interaction between his lover and his lover's wife. I could feel the vomit coming up as I thought about the things he did to me and taught me to do to him.

"Now you have someone else pregnant!" she screamed but he just shook his head. I couldn't hold it in anymore. The tears streamed down my face faster and faster as I watched the way Damon looked at them with so much hate behind his eyes but it wasn't just hate. He was hurt.

"I'm not pregnant by your husband." I said but my eyes never left Damon's face.

"Wait, what?" Teresa asked. I knew she was confused because before this very moment, I was confused too. I didn't deserve this and neither did she. I felt Arteal place her hand on my shoulder. I looked over at her and she looked like she had so much to say but she didn't utter a word. Instead she gave me a head nod.

"This baby doesn't belong to your husband."

"Well what the fuck are we here for?! See I don't have time for these childish ass high school games you little bitches playing!" Teresa snapped and I completely understood her frustrations.

James looked over at me with pleading eyes. He now knew that I knew about him and Damon. He shook his head slowly but subtly. It was his way of telling me not to do what I was about to do.

I looked back at Damon. He had tiny beads of sweat sliding down his face. Arteal threw her arm around me in a comforting way but all it did was bring her closer to me and I could smell nothing but piss.

I stepped away from her and tried to build the courage to say what needed to be said. As I stared into each of their faces, I knew that I needed to tell her or she'd never know. She had a confused angry look on her face as she waited for me to answer her question but I stood there completely stuck on stupid.

"Hello? Why am I here?" she screamed again. I could hear the librarian making her way towards the commotion. I'm surprised it took her this long to finally come check things out.

"Zaria don't do this." Damon pleaded as he looked at me. Teresa turned around and looked at Damon with a questioning look on her face. How dare he tell me not to do this! This isn't my doing, it's his and James! That statement alone was enough for me. I laughed a small laugh to myself as I stared directly at Damon.

"I'm pregnant by your husband's boyfriend."